PRISM
MOON

Martine Bates

Red Deer College Press

Copyright © 1993 Martine Bates
2nd Printing, 1998

All rights reserved. No part of this book may be reproduced by any
means, electronic or mechanical, including photography, recording,
or any information storage and retrieval system, without permission in
writing from the publisher.

Northern Lights Young Novels are published by
Red Deer College Press
56 Avenue & 32 Street Box 5005
Red Deer Alberta Canada T4N 5H5

Edited for the Press by Tim Wynne-Jones.
Cover art and design by Ron Lightburn.
Text design by Dennis Johnson.
Printed and bound in Canada by Friesen Corp.
Red Deer College Press.

The publishers gratefully acknowledge the financial assistance of the
Alberta Foundation for the Arts, the Canada Council, the Depart-
ment of Communications and Red Deer College.

Canadian Cataloguing in Publication Data
Bates, Martine, 1953–
(Northern lights young novels)
Sequel to: The dragon's tapestry.
ISBN 0-88995-095-4
I. Title. II. Series.
PS8553.A828P7 1993 jC813'.54 C92-091844-1
PZ7.B37Pr 1993

*T*o Sterling
Sarah
Rachel
Russell
Candace
and Derek,
who gave me six lessons in love.

Thanks are due to the Alberta Foundation for the Literary Arts for their financial assistance so I could write this story, and to Fenton and Kelli, who gave me the story about how the North Wind got its whistle.

The widest land
Doom takes to part us, leaves thy heart in mine
With pulses that beat double. What I do
And what I dream include thee...

ELIZABETH BARRETT BROWNING
Sonnets from the Portuguese

THE
PRISM
MOON

PROLOGUE

Bed and bower
weed and flower
moat and tower
blood and power.
—A VEAN CHILD'S NURSERY RHYME

"DO IT," MAUG SAID. "DO IT NOW."
The old woman reached a trembling hand toward the small moon that hovered spinning and sparkling in the air only an arm's length away, then retracted her hand as if it had been burnt.

"I cannot," she whispered. "I am afraid."

Maug looked at her as if he could not see her clearly. "We've planned so long, Shadrah," he said. "We've used so much of our magic to find the prism moon. Don't you think the Mother has helped us, that she wants us to take it? It is written that all will love the one who finds and touches the prism moon. Think, Shadrah, what power it will bring to the order of the Oldwives when you, as the Oldest, possess it. And it would give you power to convince the people of what you know about me."

She shook her head, her thin white hair blowing in the wind. "To touch it, yes, but to pluck it out of the sky.... It is too much for an old woman. It would be better if you ..."

Maug's body vanished, and only his head floated in the air, a leering planet to the little moon. The old woman's mouth moved in silence.

"Do you believe that I am the heir to the wizard, Shadrah?" he asked. "Do you believe your dreams?"

"Yes, Maug."

"No. You believe Marwen to be the wizard's heir. You must go to your grave with your tapestry unfulfilled, having never seen the wizard's son."

The old woman shook her head. Her young apprentice watched from a distance, stroking her black yellow-marked wingwand and licking her fingers.

"Take the moon in your hand," he said, his body becoming visible again.

Shadrah looked up slowly. Silent lightning lit the horizon in the distance as she reached her hand toward the moon. The wind blew the night air, and a cold rain began to fall.

"Fabled moon," Shadrah said into the wind, "beautiful moon of lyric legend, mythical moon ... forgive this old woman."

Her hand grasped it, and the spinning stopped. The light of the moon shone through her fingers with a blood-red glow.

Thunder rumbled in the distance, and the apprentice gripped her wingwand to keep it from bucking. Cullerwind blew up from beneath them and filled their eyes with wind and dust.

Shadrah did not move, but stood there with her right hand holding up the moon as if she were offering it to the night sky.

"Now I see what I have not seen," she said, and her voice trembled.

"Give it to me," Maug shouted above the wind. His brass-colored hair blew straight on end, and eddies of dust swirled around him.

The old woman's body shook. "I cannot let go!" she cried. The apprentice stopped licking her fingers and touched the glass knife she carried. Slowly, Shadrah lowered her arm.

She saw it once: a ball of crystal, a lump of diamond, a tiny moon gleaming with an inner light, perfect in its hard bright beauty. She saw it in her hand once, briefly, before the thin jag of lightning cracked over the hill and burst upon her forehead.

She crumpled to the earth, and Maug knelt beside the moon still gripped in the dead woman's hand.

"Come take it out of her hand for me," he said to the apprentice.

The girl approached, holding the glass knife, and stopped behind Maug. Maug curled his body over the moon. He touched it and shuddered. He tried to take it from the hand of the corpse, but the fingers would not be pried. At his gesture the apprentice fell to her knees beside the body of her mistress and, with her knife, cut away the old woman's fingers one by one. She kissed the last and put it in her tapestry pouch.

"Now you are mine," Maug whispered to the moon. "Bright heart of Ve, I hold you at last as my own, so that all I desire in the world might be mine—its love, its pleasures, and especially ..." He took the moon in his hand and looked toward the north sky. "And especially give me ... Marwen."

CHAPTER ONE

Each moon brings to earth a dowry:
from Epsilon, rain and rivers and the tides of the sea;
from Opo, fun and the protection of fools;
from Non, song and simplicity;
and from Orbica, seeds and growing things.
Clewdroin gives vision and peace,
and Globa, the jewels of the earth.
Septa brings power, bravery, and strength.
—*TENETS OF THE TAPESTRY*

THE WINGWAND CLICKED HER EXHAUS-
tion to Marwen. "Soon, Zephrelle, soon,"
Marwen said, and she slid a hand reassuringly between the
head and thorax plates of the beast's hard body. Disturbed by
Zephrelle's wingbeat, the thick white mists swirled on the tops
of the hills and dripped down the rock. Behind the foothills, in
the moonlight, Marwen could see the thin shadows of snow-
covered mountains far off, seemingly no closer than when she
and Torbil had begun their journey. Even with her wingwand,
it would be many windcycles before she reached her destination, Mt. Ornu.

She looked up. Floating in the deep sea of the heavens like
crescent boats were the seven moons of Ve: Epsilon, water-
blue mother moon; the twins, Opo and Non; Orbica, the
green and mysterious forest moon; white Clewdroin, with

Orbica hovering like a silver jewel on her face; and golden
Globa hanging rich and heavy nearest the horizon. Just crest-
ing the horizon was Septa, the largest of the moons, a broad
bold moon, a husband moon perhaps to Epsilon, big-bellied
when at its full, narrow-chested and lean now at its crescent
stage. She watched it crown, watched as its polished point lit
the horizon, dimming the stars in the east. Above her the
bright star Jersha shone milk sweet and benign in the night
sky, undimmed by the moonlight. The smaller star Jie spun
around her, less offspring than pet, a grey pup that dogged her
shining white skirts and chased its own tail and followed her
faithfully across the winter night and into the day.

Again Zephrelle clicked impatiently, and so Marwen landed
the wingwand on the flat top of the nearest hill. Tympanoo,
Torbil's mount and Zephrelle's mate, followed close behind.
Marwen pulled soft stockings over Zephrelle's antennae.

"Poor beast," Marwen said softly. "You have done bravely
today." Zephrelle collapsed to the ground exhausted and
would not graze. Her wings were as limp as white spidersilk,
her long hard body glistened in the moonbeams. She twittered
gently and with her antennae touched Marwen's long silver
braid, which was the sign of purity, of the virgin. To the south
a white vein of lightning touched the earth and, after a few
moments, another.

"Not much for them to eat around here," Torbil called
gruffly. "A few bunchberries, maybe, and some leafblack. Here,
hold on!" He was trying to groom and cover Tympanoo's
furred antennae, but the wingwand had been temperamental
and unmanageable since their journey had begun. At one point
the beast had bucked, throwing their food pack. They searched
for it, but it had fallen into a deep river, and Torbil swore the
beast had planned it so. Now Torbil and Tympanoo struggled,
and as soon as the stockings were in place, the beast butted

him, and Torbil fell. Marwen's laughter rang thinly over the fog-damp hills.

When he'd finished cursing, Torbil spread the greatrug over the brittle grass and the ground still damp from a recent upwelling.

"Why I feel hungry for them I don't know. My stomach is empty, and there's nothing for us to eat around here either," he said, rubbing his beard. "Can your magic make a meal of this?" He showed Marwen a handful of wilting leafblack.

"Torbil, I thought you were an unbeliever," Marwen said, smiling. She stroked Zephrelle. They had gone too far today, and Marwen berated herself. Tympanoo still had his strength though. He searched the hollows for food.

"Though I serve you by reason of loyalty and the orders of the Prince Camlach, I still cannot believe. Mind, if you could conjure me a nice roast callobird, I might be persuaded...."

Marwen laughed again and shook her head. "You know it is forbidden to do magic in winterdark, Torbil." She raised a finger. "But in the absence of magic, there is another power the One Mother values as highly: common sense. See what I brought?" Marwen took from her new tapestry pouch a purse of dried berries, being careful not to crush the tapestry beneath for which she had battled a dragon, the tapestry that had woven into it the sign of the staff, the symbol that was both gift and burden to Marwen.

"Ah, so you brought something. Are you sure it was not too heavy?" Torbil said.

Marwen smiled and then frowned with worry. "It is just as well. Zephrelle seemed hardly able to carry me this past wind. Do you think she is sick, Torbil?"

"Humph!" Torbil examined the hard red berries and popped one into his mouth. He promptly spat it out. "I can't eat these—they taste like rocks," Torbil grumbled in his deep gravelly voice. "Rather eat leafblack." He tore a chunk off with his teeth and chewed disconsolately.

"Take heart, Torbil," Marwen said. "In another windcycle or two, you will be with Prince Camlach and your friends, while I will be in the snow and cold of the mountains...."

Torbil spat again noisily and pointed at her with two thick calloused fingers.

"Prince Camlach will throw me in the dungeon for leaving you to go to into the mountains alone," he said. Marwen could not see his dark bearded face at all, even in the moonlight. He drew out of his quiver an arrow and began picking the leafblack out of his teeth with its point. "Use some of that common sense, Marwen. Come with me to Camlach, and we will take you later to Mt. Ornu. This is a magic I can believe in," and he patted his quiver.

"No, I can't wait any longer," she said.

"The prince gave me strict instructions...."

"To obey me," she said.

"To protect you," he said. "Must I force you?"

"What do they say the wizard does to those who displease her?"

Torbil chewed while he spoke. "Nurse told me when I was a child that the wizard turned bad boys into wartwiggles."

"Wartwiggles," Marwen nodded, "or worse."

"And so I would ask nurse, 'How is it then that there are so many bad boys in Ve?'"

"And what did she answer?"

"Punished wartwiggles." Torbil winked at Opo, the moon of fun and protection of fools. Still, Marwen didn't laugh. She looked toward the shadow-mountains, pale and cold in the half-light of winterdark. Deep in those mountains lived the Staffmaker. He alone could fashion the staff that would give her the full powers of the wizard.

"I can't wait any longer, Torbil," she said. It was not only her urgency to have her staff that made her firm. Every day she had known it was wrong to delay looking for Maug. Somewhere, if he lived, he had no tapestry. She knew what that was like; it was to make an hour too long, a day unbearable. "Besides, who is to say that Prince Camlach even thinks of me."

"His message was, 'Come and bring Marwen.' That sounds clear enough to me."

Marwen was running her hand over Zephrelle's legs, feeling for ulcers or sign of parasites. She stopped and looked up. "Before that he said he would come with me to seek my staff. He did not come. Well, I must go in any case. Now that he may be King someday, perhaps it is not possible for him to love someone like me."

Torbil shook his head. "That could be rumor. No word comes from the prince about this. No news comes about what has happened to his older brother." He swung his great shaggy head sorrowfully. "If you knew Prince Ronor as I do, you would mourn with me." Torbil's fist closed over his arrow. "Your magic tells you nothing? What is it to be a wizard anyway, Marwen? In the past few months, you have been sought out by people wishing for a shorter nose or a new wife or a bag of gold. All of them you send back to their Oldwife, even the shorter-nose people—you do not laugh at them—back to the Oldwife. Is this the work of a wizard? What is it about this stick that will make you weightier on the scales of the One Mother?"

No, she did not laugh at the girl who'd come to her for a shorter nose or at the mother who knew she'd be happy forever if only she had a pot that never burned the stew or the farmer who needed a fatter heartier seed. She didn't laugh. Marwen knew what it was to want, to want so badly that you were afraid to say it out loud and to believe that all the gets

and haves in the world could never balance out the want. It
was that way with her staff. It was that way with her prince.

"The staff symbol is in my tapestry. That is reason enough
to seek the staff, is it not?" She coaxed Zephrelle to her feet
and led her to the tender grass Tympanoo had found in a hollow. Then she sat beside Torbil and ripped a handful of grass.

"There is great evil in the world that you do not see," he
said. "I worry."

Marwen laughed and threw the grass at him.

"Torbil, you worry all the time. You worry about me and
Camlach and everyone in between. You worry about the
upwellings, too little this day, too much that day, and the
winds, how they blow differently than last winterdark. You
worry the cream into cheese, just like an old grandmother.
How can you forget that I banished a dragon?"

Instantly, she felt ashamed for mentioning this. It was not
what an Oldwife would say, much less an Oldwife who sought
a wizard's staff.

"You brag like an old grandmother," Torbil said, obviously
stung. "You think of the evil of a dragon as a great thing. But
there is greater evil than that—there is the evil found in men."

"I have never seen such a thing."

"No? What of your cousin Maug?"

Marwen snorted. "Maug was a boy. My own age. How do
you know of him?"

"Camlach warned me of him once. And I have heard you
say his name in your sleep."

Marwen lay back on the greatrug. "I will tell you about
Maug," she said, invoking the storyspell. She wasn't very good
at the storyspell. Even people with no magic at all did better
than she, round their fires at night. But she had been practicing
since winterdark descended, when it was the only spell permit-
ted.

She began telling how Maug had hated her when they were young and how he, besides herself, had been the sole survivor of the burning of Marmawell. She told how he had tried to keep her from confronting the dragon Perdoneg, and so she was forced to leave him in the wilderness to find the Oldest on his own, and how she had promised to come as soon as she could to witness for his tapestry, which had been burned by the dragon....

"You forgot the part when he stole Politha's magical coverlet," Torbil interrupted.

Marwen sat up. "You're not supposed to be able to speak or move. I was making a storyspell," she said.

Torbil looked confused. "Oh."

Marwen sighed and Torbil said, "It wasn't so bad. Keep on."

"It isn't that. It's this promise I made to Maug. How could I have let him go so long without keeping my promise? No, I know why. I was afraid."

"Why were you afraid?"

Marwen looked down. "I don't know."

"You are afraid that he is dead?"

"I am afraid that he is alive," Marwen said.

Torbil looked at her, and his black eyes reflected the starlight. "You, Marwen, who defeated a dragon, who ventures into mountains alone, you are afraid of a boy with whom you grew up?"

Marwen smiled at his teasing and then looked away.

She had never known anyone so consumed with anger as Maug, except perhaps his mother, Merva, who seemed to have hated her before she was born. She did not tell Torbil of the vivid dream she had been having, the same dream, more than once, in which Nimroth her father was comforting a woman. At first she thought it was her mother, but then she knew the woman was Merva. In the most recent dream, he had been saying something, but Marwen could not hear the words. In every sleeping wind, Marwen woke up sweating.

"Before I seek him, to do his tapestry, I will gain strength in my staff," she said to Torbil.

She remembered how Maug's anger had seethed under his skin always, bubbling up at times like unstirred yeast. But Maug was her cousin; Merva had been her aunt: family. She thought of those who had journeyed to repeople that which had once been Marmawell—young families disillusioned with their parents' way of life, who thought it would be better to plant spice gardens than herd goats or spin thread, old families who sought a drier warmer climate to relieve their bone disease, families with many children, who ran away from something: a memory, a debt, themselves. She had marveled at these families as they came to her to pay their respects. They were little tribes: two-people, ten-people tribes that kept their love quiet or secret, Marwen could not tell which. She knew, though, that all the magic in the world could not buy it or wish it. There was no spell for it, save the slow one that was worked each morning over the porridge pot, each night beside the fire, each plodding day. And so Marwen dreamed of a staff that stood straight and tall as a father, that listened to deep dreams, good and bad, like a sister, that granted wishes like a mother. But in between, like a bad note on a cupplehorn, the other dream played.

In the hollows the fog lay light and still and knee-deep. The wingwands' heads disappeared when they dipped them to graze. She nudged Torbil.

"Do you think a wizard could do such a thing? Make a nose shorter, I mean. It would be a tricky spell, shortening the nose just the right amount, without shortening the whole face or making one cross-eyed. After I have my staff, I must try. Of course, I'd have to try it on myself first."

Torbil laughed, a round ringing laugh that scattered the mists settling in their laps and startled the wingwands. They twittered uneasily and waved their antennae. Then for a time there was silence, and the mists again began to settle on their skins, damp and cold.

"I should go," he said.

"Yes," she said.

He did not move.

"Are there no beautiful women in Duma for you to return to, Torbil?" Marwen teased.

"All women are beautiful in winterdark," Torbil said distractedly.

It was part of a proverb, but Marwen could not remember the rest of it. Camlach had once thought her pretty in summersun. Would he think her beautiful in winterdark? Why hadn't he come? "Still," Torbil said, and his head hung huge and dark, "still, I cannot go without you."

"You think I can't do it alone, don't you. I am fullnamed and sixteen suns. That is old enough to fulfill my tapestry."

She knew Torbil would think of Perdoneg, who ruled the land of the lost, that twilight land where go the souls of those whose tapestries are not fulfilled. He would remember the fires of the dragon. She watched his eyes close against the memory.

He stood up, nodding heavily.

"Well," he said. "Well. You vanquished a dragon. Some might say it was only with a good bit of luck, of course, but no doubt you are not the ordinary maiden that you look. Have you a message for Prince Camlach?"

Marwen smoothed the grass with her hand and let the dry tips tickle her palm. "Yes. Tell him ... tell him that my memories of him burn like dragon fire.... No. No, tell him rather to fix a day in winterdark when I may come and show him my staff. No ... tell him nothing."

Torbil made a grunting sound and was shouldering his quiver when he stopped. He looked back at Marwen as if she were a ghost and then past her to the south.

"What is it?" she asked. She could hear nothing but the sound of cullerwind, that brief battering wind, as it began to blow over the hills.

"What, Torbil?"

He pointed. Marwen felt the magic prickle under her skin. She stood and turned in one movement.

Far to the south, the sky was lit brightly as the lightning storm became more violent. All around them cullerwind shredded the soft mists into rags and phantoms. Just as their view became clear, a thin jag of lightning cracked lengthwise across the mountains and the darkness, and touched the earth far away. Cullerwind died and the lightning stopped. A heavier darkness settled over them, and a deeper silence.

Marwen stood still on the hilltop, facing south. "It was only a lightning storm, Torbil," she said, but the resettling mists seemed to muffle her words. She was unsure if he had heard. In the fragments of falling mist, Marwen was seeing a vision, a shadow of herself standing in a high place, gazing over and past rivers to a bitter cold sea. Something sank into a dark pool of water or sky, sank fast, leaving only the moons and stars reflected, but changed. No longer did the constellations of the Dagger, the Wheel, and the Lantern pattern the sky, but strange cold stars with no names.

"Winterdark," Torbil said softy behind her.

She turned around to face him, shivering in the cold.

"Torbil?"

"It is winterdark," he said, and his eyes were black stars. "In winterdark you are nothing more than an ordinary young maiden, for you can work no magic. I will not leave you. You must come with me."

"Torbil, you are swayed by a lightning storm as a child would be," she chided, but she felt the wind cold on her back. Something ... There was something....

"It is a portent," he said.

"It is a storm, Torbil. Nothing else."

"You must come with me," he said.

"I must seek my staff."

He stood adamant, his legs spread, his hands fisted. "The prince commanded me to serve you."

"If you are my servant, then obey me and go," Marwen said.

Torbil blinked, and his arms hung heavily at his sides. Marwen was shaking. Never had she commanded him before. The wind sounded like a whistle in her ears, and Marwen looked up to see if one of the moons spun faster than before.

"Torbil, I'm sorry. You are my friend...."

But if he heard her, she could not tell, for in the next moment, he had mounted Tympanoo and was urging him skyward. Before he was out of sight, Tympanoo realized that Zephrelle was not coming behind, and he screamed for her. Zephrelle screamed in reply, her covered antennae waving powerlessly. Soon the whole earth seemed to ring with screams, but Marwen could see nothing but the black silent sky to the south.

CHAPTER TWO

The gifts of the younger moons—bravery, vision,
or song—may be withheld, may be just out of
reach of the Mother's children. But the unseen
moon is close to the earth, and her gift is for all,
even the silent creatures.
—FROM *THE LATER WRITINGS OF MARWEN OF MAR-
MAWELL*

*T*HE JOURNEY TOOK MARWEN AWAY FROM
the dry temperate inlands, where Marmawell
had been rebuilt, toward a cold sea that dumped heavy fogs
and snows on its shores. But before the sea were the coastal
mountains of the Eastsea Range. Mt. Ornu was at its edge.
That was all she knew. It was enough. She knew that if she had
to she could smell her way to the magic of the Staffmaker.

Zephrelle was unable to fly more than two winds now without stopping to rest. Marwen stopped at a village called Chi-
tinick, known for its brasswork and potmaking, and again at
the village of Answered Corners. To both places minstrels had
traveled, and Marwen's name was known, so she was treated
with respect and fed well, though with the curiosity and care-
lessness of unbelievers. Strangely, in both villages the Oldwives
had been unable to greet her, being busy at difficult births. She

had wanted to ask for help for Zephrelle, but she left without meeting them.

When she left Answered Corners, it was with no reassurance that more villages were between there and her destination. She ventured into an unmapped land, the villagers had said, a land of rocks and bogs and boiling rivers, and at last the snowbound mountains. Marwen flew on under the moonlight, singing against the silence.

Let one who seeks great magic, lo,
see and know the winter. Go,
let him see the darkness. No,
let him find the darkness. So,
to one who seeks great magic, wo.

"Ah, Zephrelle, what a mournful verse," she said, and she began to sing the most cheerful tune she could remember.

My auntie is a janglearm, flutterlash,
ringyfinger lady,
Her daughter is a lacygown, silverspoon,
ribboncurly baby,
Her brother is a flapperjacket, toughypunch,
climbycuss boyo,
And he has a buzzyspin, boucytoss,
funnyface toyo....

It seemed that the wind thickened and resisted her. Zephrelle, after only one wind's flight, was already tired. Short of using her magic, she had done everything she could to help the beast, not knowing what the trouble was. There seemed no sickness on her at all. In the back of Marwen's brain, she began to feel that it was her fault, that she was heavier, that her heart was collapsing like an old star, becoming dense and dark and hard. The winter darkness confused her, and she had to use a point on the horizon, rather than the stars, to navigate her way.

"Moon madness," she said aloud.

In a dark valley Marwen landed the beast away from the sight of stars and sky. Only prickly weeds emerged from the dry stony soil, but Zephrelle seemed uninterested in grazing anyway. Marwen groomed Zephrelle's antennae and long back hair with slow heavy movements. She too was tired. She felt as if a huge hand were pressing her down, as if she held up the sky with her shoulders.

"Lovely beast," Marwen said softly. "Soon you will carry on your back the wizard of Ve. Just be brave and carry me to the Staffmaker. He will help you to be well." Her voice sounded tiny in the valley, like a single bean rolling in a big pot, and she spoke louder. "What do you think the Staffmaker will ask of me, Zephrelle? The staff is not a gift, you know. A price is demanded, a price most particularly suited to the one desiring it."

She holstered the grooming brush and opened her tapestry pouch. Inside, besides her tapestry, a whitesoap wingwand, and the depleted bag of berries, was a carefully wrapped book, a journal her wizard father had kept and which she had found in the spring beneath his house. Though she had poured laboriously over the thin script, she still had not read it all, and she hoped the Staffmaker would not demand it of her. It was almost all she owned in the world, except for the dragon's tapestry buried safely in the hills of Marmawell, and except for Zephrelle.

A gift from Camlach, the wingwand had become more than beast, more even than pet. In her gentle twitterings, Marwen had understood the wingwand's intelligence and love. She would mourn many days were the Staffmaker to ask for her wingwand. She stood and poured the remaining berries near the wingwand, having lost her own appetite at the thought of it. Zephrelle breathed uneasily and ignored the berries, so Marwen fed them to her one by one. When the last was gone, Zephrelle slept.

Thoughtfully, Marwen undid her knee-length braid to comb her hair. She hated combing it, for it pulled and pinched and ripped at her scalp, and she had no patience for being gentle. Her adoptive mother, Grondil, had been careful with her tangles, had brushed and braided her hair into heavy ropes of silver, but Marwen had chafed under the comb, impatient to run away and let her hair fly in the wind. Camlach had loved her hair, and she pretended that he watched while she brushed it. "Whatever the Staffmaker asks of me, Zephrelle, it will teach me much about my tapestry, and myself. It is said that the greater the price, the greater the power of the wizard, though sacrifice to one is easy giving to another." She paused in her combing. Zephrelle snored. "I wonder what my father was required to give."

Her hair fell like molten moonlight and was lifted by the wind like a gleaming silver cape. For a few quiet moments, she let the wind move her hair, touch her arms, her fingers, her face, like light kisses, before she braided it again. She played a game with herself, one that Grondil said she had sung when she was a little girl, and one her mother had sung before her: a number for each link in her hair, beginning at twenty, for her braid reached to her hips. Twenty-three, he loves you; twenty-four means twins; twenty-five means riches; twenty-six means bad luck; twenty-seven means the Mother watches over.... But Marwen had run out of hair, and she pulled tight to make the twenty-seventh link. She shrugged and smiled.

She spread the greatrug, hugged her cloak around her tightly, and gave herself up to the lightness of sleep. She dreamed of Merva when she was beautiful, before bitterness had stitched her face up too tight with flesh-colored threads. Nimroth spoke to her, his voice soft as cloth, his words sure and fine as a good needle—but she could not hear him.

SHE WAS AWAKENED by a pealing scream, the cry of an animal in death or terrible pain. In one heartbeat she knew it was Zephrelle.

She jumped to her feet, her hands poised for spellweaving, forgetting the dark. A moment later she dropped her hands and tried to calm the magic that was sparking and snapping and surging through her body. Zephrelle's antennae drooped and quivered.

"Zephrelle, what is it?" she cried. "This is no sickness I know." Marwen knelt before her and stroked her antennae. The creature twittered weakly and then screamed again, lifting her white wings.

Marwen placed her hand on Zephrelle's head.

Fully awake now, she stilled the magic in her, knowing she dared not use it in the dark. She listened carefully to the wing-wand as it clicked and cried out. She could smell no sickness, just washes of pain in rhythmic waves. Zephrelle screamed again, a high-pitched whistle that shook with agony. Then her body relaxed into a telling stillness, and her legs folded beneath her.

Marwen knew then what racked the beast. Stroking her all the while, she walked around her.

There beside the wingwand's tail was a transparent gelatinous ball, still slick: a wingwand egg.

Marwen clapped her hands and hooted like a child.

"A baby for you, Zephrelle!" she cried. "How could I not have known?" Marwen knelt down and picked up the egg. She carried it to Zephrelle's face, to put it before her eyes. But as she knelt, Marwen saw that the starluster was gone from the beast's eyes, and her antennae were limp and cold. Zephrelle was dead.

CHAPTER THREE

Winterdark is the season of madness and love.
—Songs of the One Mother

MARWEN WAITED THERE IN THE wound of the hills for many winds until the body of Zephrelle had begun to stink and poisonous iplizards came scavenging for the meat.

After she spread her greatrug over the wingwand's body, she began to walk, carrying the egg in her arms like a child. It was heavy, but not as heavy as it should have been for it was premature. In the warmth of her arms it would grow. She grieved for Zephrelle, wished she had had the knowledge to save her, and punished herself with the weight of the egg. She felt a small pain in her heart like a sting: was the One Mother punishing her? Marwen knew that the One Mother had wanted her to reweave Maug's tapestry first, before seeking her staff. There was some important reason ... but Marwen had promised herself, "After, after I have my staff."

The fog swirled around Marwen's knees, pooling in the hollows, and she thought she heard a wingwand scream far away. It was wrong to have told Torbil how brave she was to have faced a dragon, not because she bragged, but because she was not brave at all. Seeing evil so close then had made her want to gather her magic around her like a nest, to make for herself a soft place where she could hide and sit on her heart's loves like eggs that never hatched. She had not been able to do it in Marmawell, where Grondil's voice sang in the barrows, where the wind was full of voices all flying away from her, where Camlach never came. And then had come the dream. Marwen had not tried to decipher the dream, but the last time she'd had it, she'd begun packing to seek her staff.

The egg was heavy, and she sat down on a rock. She felt lonely and foolish and hungry. She wished, almost, that she had followed Torbil to Camlach.

Camlach.

Marwen tried to pierce the darkness with her eye and see a castle half a world away and within it a prince. Never before had she felt the pull of the moons in the tides of her own blood as she did now. She shook her head as if to clear it.

Nuwind began to blow the damp mists away, and for the first time, Marwen could see how the countryside had changed. She had come to the end of the rolling hills and grassy hollows, and the mountains loomed ahead like gods.

Below and before the mountains stretched a marshland, flat, flooded, and reed-tufted. A vapor hung over much of it, and nuwind caused wisps of the vapor to blow upward like putrid breaths. Marwen's rock was between two streaks of water, too shallow to be brooks or streams, that ran in rivulets down the hillside, intersecting each other back and forth like a braid until they disappeared into the bogland. Wearily, she walked to the streak of water nearby and put a hand in it to drink.

VICTORIA SCHOOL LIBRARY
10830 - 103 AVENUE
EDMONTON, ALBERTA T5H 1A8

It was hot! The vapor in the valley below, Marwen realized, was steam rising from the waters of the marsh. She had heard of this land, had known of sick folk who came to bathe in the waters in the months of summersun. There seemed to be no one now; she could see no village, hear no visitors. Then she could hear their ghosts moaning and praying in the pools that gather among the reeds, and the silence rang heavier over the hills.

She hefted the egg and walked down the slope toward a thick-fogged corner of the valley, where a few huts might possibly be hidden. The ground under the thin grass was damp, and in places where she stepped, the mud oozed into her shoes. At one point in the darkness, she stopped before a pool emanating a damp warmth. In the moonlight she could see that it was funnel-shaped, and at the bottom was a deep dark hole. Marwen was strangely fascinated, unreasonably afraid. She could hardly breath in the heat of it. She walked around it uneasily.

Before she was close enough to the fog-held corner of the valley to see if any houses were there, her clothes were drenched, and her legs weary and her arms aching from the weight of Zephrelle's egg.

She sat on a dry knoll to rest, nestling the egg in her lap. She sat a long time before she noticed the little creatures that crept upon her spidersilk and covered her shoes. She stood up and stifled a shudder of disgust. She was an Oldwife and the wizard's heir. All creatures were her stewardship. All life belonged to the Mother, she told herself quietly, as she removed them one by one and put them gently on the ground with trembling fingers.

"Strong little wet bodies without much of a brain," she said to herself, and her words fell soft and muffled into the mists. "How like the Mother to plant the seeds of life even here."

"Even here? What do you mean 'even here'?" a voice said from the darkness.

Marwen started. She forgot the wormlike creatures and looked up into the face of an old woman dressed in blue spidersilk. In the moonlight and the mists, she looked like a ghost.

"Welcome, stranger, to the land of boiling wells and spidersilk larvae."

The woman was hunched and saggy, and her face was as wrinkled as brothbreads, but her black eyes were sharp and knowing, and her bottom lip poked out amazingly far. Marwen stared at the slippery inside of her lip and could not speak.

"Visitors should watch how they speak about these marshlands. These marshlands belong to me and my people," the old woman said.

"By what authority?" Marwen said, recovering herself, remembering that she was the wizard's heir.

"By forfeit," the old woman said, and she cackled uproariously, slapping her thighs. Her loose belly swayed beneath her spidersilk, and her large breasts, which sagged to her waist, shook. "Seldom do visitors come, always do they leave. Quickly." She snapped the last word, and Marwen jumped back.

"Well, then, I will not surprise you by being any different," Marwen said, and she gathered the egg into her arms.

"What is that?" the old woman asked.

"It is a wingwand egg."

The old woman stared. "Wingwands do not live here easily," she said. "Where are you going?"

Marwen nodded her head toward the mountains. The woman said nothing, and Marwen turned to leave.

"Wait," the old woman said. Her voice had softened.

Marwen stopped. Her chest hurt. She was not afraid now, only weary and hungry, and the blood weighed heavy in her heart. The old woman was peering closely at her and glanced several times at the mountains. Her lip moved as though she were trying to remember something.

"You are gentle with the little creatures of the swamp and respectful of unborn life," she said at last. "I perceive that you have a long journey ahead. I invite you to eat with us if you will, and I will give you provisions to take with you. There is nothing to eat in the mountains."

There was a pleading edge to her voice, a hidden hope in the cupping of her stiff old hands.

Marwen's stomach grumbled loudly enough so the old woman had surely heard.

"I am Bashag," she said, gesturing to Marwen to follow. "Bashag Oldwife."

"I didn't know," Marwen said, stuttering slightly. "Bashag Oldwife, let your hands be blessed...."

"Nonsense. None of that," she said.

"But the books say ..."

Bashag laughed. "We don't stand on the rule book much around here—make it so you can fall off." Bashag laughed again. "What is your name?"

"Marwen. Of Marmawell."

Bashag's bottom lip poked out again, and the muscles of her neck strained when she peered more closely into Marwen's face. Then she nodded and mumbled something and gestured to Marwen to follow her. She walked quickly for one of her age, and it was all Marwen could do to keep up. After a time she began to speak, and at first Marwen thought she was talking to herself.

"First there was Janfa, who died in childbirth, and then Vastia, the wife of the clan chief, who gave birth to a stillborn son. That was three days ago. Last weswind Cilandra of a connected clan gave birth to a male child so malformed it soon died. During this time I have pled for the One Mother to send you. She answered quickly."

"I am sorry, I don't understand," Marwen said, walking heavily with the egg in her arms.

Bashag stopped. She came very close to Marwen, and Marwen could smell snowseed on her—snowseed that is ground and used to ease fever and pain. Her grey hair blew in dry stiff shreds around her face, but it was clean, and her spidersilk was clean and beautifully woven.

"Are you not the wizard's heir?" Bashag whispered, peering into Marwen's face. "Marwen of Marmawell? She who interprets the dragon's tapestry?"

Marwen said nothing, strangely suspicious of the old woman. Bashag nodded sharply. "Aye, I thought so. We have asked the Mother to send you, we have. She listens. She waits on one's belief. Then she gives. Let it always be so." Again the old woman began walking, gesturing impatiently for Marwen to walk more quickly. Marwen had to stride to keep up.

"My young apprentice knew of you. We have waited and hoped you would come. Just this norwind Manora cast off the child within her, and much blood. The gleaning has grown thin of late but not so much as to cause this. I have been Oldwife since Shadrah was young, and never have I seen what I see now."

"Shadrah? The Oldest?" Marwen asked, panting.

"Yes." Bashag stopped so suddenly that Marwen almost bumped into her. Her whole chin seemed covered by that huge pouting lower lip, glistening and blue-veined. "She is dead you know."

Marwen forgot the weight of the egg for a moment. "How do you know this?" she asked.

"My apprentice," Bashag answered. "She came from Loobhan only a short time ago with the news. She agreed to stay and work for me for a time—I was pleased for she has a great talent. It was her idea, in fact, to pray you here."

"When did Shadrah die?" Marwen asked.

"Not long ago, at the first rising of Septa," Bashag said.

Marwen's arms ached with the weight of the egg, the weight of Zephrelle's baby. Perhaps the death of the Oldest explained the thickness of the air in her lungs of late, the strange discomfort in the bottom of her stomach.

"This I have known in my heart, but my head would not hear it," Marwen said. "Then even more reason to continue my journey to the mountains."

"You seek the Staffmaker, then?" Bashag asked.

Marwen glanced at her. "You are wise in the lore."

"I am," the old woman nodded solemnly, and Marwen smiled in spite of her aching arms. "I think my apprentice is wiser than I, but even she cannot tell me why we are losing this harvest of children. You must help us."

"I will try," Marwen said, but her mouth felt dry, and the magic seemed far from her. She followed Bashag through waist-high swamp grass and meadows of mud, closer to the first of the mountains.

Just when Marwen thought she must drop the egg in exhaustion, Bashag pointed and said, "There."

It was a large village, the homes built not of straw bricks, as in Marmawell, but of reeds and grasses and mud, and they were raised on stilts. Around each house was a matted platform, and joining each house to another were narrow straw-woven bridges. Marwen saw young children jumping lightly across the bridges, and women also, their long skirts overhanging the edges so that they appeared to float in the air. They were a tall dark people.

"Wreathen-Rills it is called," the old woman said. "Known in Ve for fine spidersilk. Come, my home is over there."

Bashag's home was in the middle of the village, and bridges sprang from it as though it were the center of a great web. Through the east window of every home, Marwen could see huge looms and upon them reams of spidersilk draped like waterfalls of color.

Here were not the small inkle looms of Oldwives, but large looms with shuttles as tall as a man and four heddles operated by footlams. She caught glimpses of men and women passing the shuttle, weaving the weft with quick graceful movements, bubbling the weft into place with the small pointed bones of animals, slamming the beater between the cloth and the reed. Bashag would explain that each loom had its own name, that each bolt of cloth was considered a noble work, and weaving a labor like childbirth. The rhythms of the whispering shuttles, the creaking of the heddlebeams, comforted Marwen's heart.

"I have never seen the spidersilk made," Marwen said in wonder, and the old woman chuckled and nodded. There were no chimneys in the houses. Between the bridges Marwen could see women working around huge metal pots suspended over natural hot pools that bubbled and boiled. Men and children, waiting in line with bowls in hand, turned to stare as Marwen passed.

On a slope to the west of the village, a single wingwand grazed, a huge black-winged beast with bright yellow wing markings.

Bashag led her up a small ladder onto the platform and into her home. While Marwen's eyes were still adjusting to the light of a large glowfly crystal, Bashag knelt and began plucking from her dress and shoes the wormlike creatures that still clung to her. A clay pot was in a corner of the house, and into this Bashag dropped the worms.

"These are the larvae that make the spidersilk," Bashag explained to Marwen. "We honor them, for they give us the beautiful textiles that we trade for metals and other things not easily found in the swamplands. Had you destroyed them, as most visitors do, the spirits of the swamp would have been angry, and they would have made your way through the swamp dangerous at best. But you did not, and I welcome you, Marwen, wizard's heir, to my home."

It was a charming home, bright with the colorful cloth that abounded in Wreathen-Rills and the clutter of the weaver's craft: a quill wheel, shuttles with runes carved into the bone of them, niddy-noddies, heddle frames, swifts, harnesses, carders, heaps of spidersilk thread, many-sized spools of twine. Everywhere were cushions, like strewn petals, and dishes of flowers: creamleaf, dewcup, and dragon teas. A basket was filled with papers of bright needles and hundreds of buttons, none of them round, but all of odd shapes. A broom stood in its spot against the wall, tricky as a hearthcat, and beside it, a painted clay chamber pot.

"Where is your husband?" Marwen asked.

Bashag chuckled. "I am married to the magic, child. It feeds me like a husband, comes to me at night—that is why I found you. I often walk the marshes in winterdark and spend my magic into the warm wells. It is good two ways: in summersun the sick come and are healed in the waters, and also it is harder for me to make winterdark magic by mistake. Here, I have something for you."

Bashag disappeared and returned shortly with a dress of white spidersilk in her arms.

"This is a gift to the wizard's heir from me and my apprentice. Try it on. We made it to assure the One Mother of my belief that you would come. Of course, my apprentice knew."

Even draped over Bashag's arm it was lovely. Marwen shed her cloak and her grey sheath and pulled the dress over her head. It was long to the ankles and slit to the thighs for wingwand riding; the sleeves were plain and to her wrists, and the neckline was a simple line beneath her throat. Marwen had only worn undyed grey before this, and she laughed with pleasure.

"I look like a bride," she said, smoothing the silky stuff over her hips. "But I cannot take this." As she wore it, she became aware of where it touched her skin and that her skin did not forget its touch like it had with her old sheath.

"You must take it, or my apprentice will be offended," Bashag said. Her bottom lip quivered, and Marwen could see that it was covered by a web of blue veins. "Besides, this grey sheath is too small for you; it binds upon your breasts and shows too much leg." Bashag smiled. "You do look like a bride, like someone in love."

Marwen felt her face flush hot. She wanted to take it off. It was making her stomach ill to wear it. But she knew by the light in the old woman's eyes that to do so would be wrong. Marwen smiled and thanked her.

"You aren't to be married, are you?" Bashag asked with a sharp look.

"No."

"Good," she said. "I've told many a town lass, 'Don't you wed too soon, for it's slave work being a wife, and it'll stunt your growth.' Do they listen to me? Nay. 'But I am in love, Bashag,' they say, all dreamy and disgusting. Soon enough they come to me and say, 'You are wise, Bashag.' Ah, but they grow in their hearts for the hard work of love, and the very ones I told not to do it are the ones I love best. Here, eat."

Bashag fed Marwen from a pot of hot soup that had been left at her doorway and some cakes that were mildly sweet and crunchy. When Marwen was finished eating, Bashag produced a bowl of water, steaming and fragrant. With gentle caressing motions, she ministered to the young girl's feet, and while she did so, she sang an ancient song of love, a romantic tale of fair Princess Gaya and her answer to her suitor, the handsome young Barad.

> *And to him on bended knee, she said:*
> *I have seen this lake, my prince,*
> *burning gold in sunlight,*
> *edged by a gentle wood,*
> *with droll-faced flowers*
> *among the bracken*
> *and the smell of trees and grasses*
> *in the wind.*
>
> *But it is as my winter lake*
> *that I will prize it most,*
> *when I come at night.*
>
> *Then I will walk the beaches of snow,*
> *and the dark wind will make a singing quiet,*
> *and the sea will come from frozen shores*
> *to my winter lake.*
>
> *And on bended knee he answered her,*
> *It shall be so.*
> *And they were wed.*

Marwen and Bashag sang together into windeven, and Marwen learned much from the woman's knowledge of the Songs. That night Marwen dreamed of a moonboat scudding across a dark ocean, herself in white spidersilk and newly beaten gold floating after, reaching out to it. It would take her to the heights and depths and ends of the universe when she grasped its bright sides, when she climbed aboard its cup and bowl beauty.

But in her dreams a spell wrenched her. She saw that the

moons were all grey rock and cold airless winds, that Camlach was the king of them all, and he would not have her.

She woke with a cry.

The glowfly crystals had been covered. Wyxwind, the sleeping wind, blew quietly in through the east window. Marwen put her shaking hand on the warm egg beside her. Everything was silent and grey-dark. The moons cast crisscross shadows through the windows. Bashag, on the greatrug across the room, stirred. "What is it, child?" she whispered.

"Bashag ..."

"Are you well?" The old woman crossed the room on hands and knees, a black shadow against the grey ones.

Marwen lay still, afraid to move. Her voice trembled as she spoke: "Bashag, some days ago, there was a storm. I felt something.... The sky was so dark." Marwen swallowed hard. The horror of the dream was still upon her. "I know the task of that darkness, now; I know its name. Magic."

"You have had a bad dream," Bashag said, and she put her strong healer's hand on Marwen's forehead.

Marwen grasped her hand.

"No, Bashag. Not just a dream, a warning. Someone has put a spell on me."

They were both whispering.

"But who could put a spell on the wizard?" Bashag asked, relenting. Her hand grasped Marwen's hand in an equal need.

"I am not yet the wizard, Bashag. First I must obtain my staff." Marwen sat up as if she would go then, in that moment, but Bashag gently pushed her down again.

"First you must sleep. Even the wizard's heir must renew the body, the house of the soul. When the sleeping winds are done, there will be time enough for dreams and spells of darkness." She spoke the spell all mothers know and sing to their children at night, and touched her temples once, twice, three times. Marwen gave herself up to a restless sleep. One time she woke briefly and saw that Bashag watched out the window until the waking winds blew.

CHAPTER FOUR

Dreams are the conversation of spirits: the One
Mother to the mortal, the dead to the living, or
the hidden self to the seen self.
—*TENETS OF THE TAPESTRY*

T HE FEAR WAS STILL THERE, LIKE A COLD
worm in Marwen's stomach, when she first
awoke, but it eased in the room awash with light from the
uncovered glowfly crystals. Beside Marwen's greatrug was a
bowl of steaming porridge.

Bashag was grinding roots with pestle and bowl. Beside her,
draped in cloth like a bony old woman, sat her loom. Bashag
was talking to it.

"I know. Don't think I don't know. I have work to do.
Shush. Shush, I say. There is work, and then there is work, my
dear, and I have chosen a warm one today. Save you and the
spinning for another day. Oh!"

Marwen sat up.

"I heard you talking to your loom," she said, rubbing her
eyes.

Bashag concentrated on her work. "Well, you might have been dreaming, lass," she said. "No one would believe you. But if it is true, and no one's saying it is, there is great magic in the loom, and it is wise to make a friend of it. It is the tool the One Mother used to make the earth and the heavens—how else do you suppose they all stick together, the moons, the stars? Why don't they all fly off like bubbles? Because they are bound, child, like thread on the Mother's loom." The woman put her fingers to her lips and then to her loom. "I was just making up a bit of a brew here for Loronda, who's due to have her baby at the next deep breath."

She went back to her task and began to hum the Song of Princess Gaya and Prince Barad.

Marwen plucked nervously at the new white spidersilk. She felt suddenly sorrowed by a song that had often brought her joy. She shivered violently and looked out the east window at the stars. Yes, the dream spoke true. There was a spell. The spell took everything that was good and lovely, and twisted it into something dark and cold. The stars spun themselves into silver streaks, and Marwen covered her eyes with her hands.

It came to her that she should feel ashamed, being abed when her hostess was already at work, and she rose and washed and swept the broken threads from under the loom before she ate. Bashag ate with her, quiet and thoughtful. The song of the famous lovers still filled Marwen's ears.

"Bashag, what is love?" Marwen asked, poking at her porridge. She made her voice light and brave. She was embarrassed that she had awoken the old woman in the night with a bad dream like a child.

The old woman chuckled kindly. "You must ask one wiser than I," she answered. "Eat quickly. My apprentice has asked that she might meet you."

But the question Marwen had asked lightly, halfheartedly,

now seemed important, and she would not be put off.

"Can love that is true be broken by a spell?" she asked, swirling the warm cream.

"I think not," Bashag said. "Though perhaps a spell could weaken a half-formed love, the bud of the flower."

Marwen stared straight down into the bowl, through the steam.

"How can I give my heart when I am unsure of how it will be treated?" she asked.

The old woman fed the fire and poked at it. "You speak as one who is afraid and beset by doubts. A better question is this: what will you do with the heart that is entrusted to you? Will you slake your own passions and give your own heart first blood, leaving the other to die? Rather, say you love for love's sake, because you choose to love. Then will your love last into death's lands, and death will not cause you to forget each other's face." She put down her bowl. "You fear your love."

The porridge slopped off Marwen's spoon. She said "No" in her mind, and "What love?" but truth had been trained into her tongue at Grondil's knee, and she said, "I think it must be the spell that makes me doubt."

Bashag was silent, and then she said, "I feel no spell, though many would have an interest in keeping an unnamed wizard from her staff. Perhaps you should beware of that which is in yourself."

Just then the dark-haired head of a man appeared in the east window.

"Bashag Oldwife, let your hands be blessed. Loronda Toy-maker labors in childbirth. Come quickly."

"Have you called my apprentice?" Bashag asked, dropping her spoon.

"She is there already."

"Come," Bashag said to Marwen. Marwen stopped to pick

up the egg. She would not chance leaving Zephrelle's baby out of her sight.

"Now you will see with your own eyes what has been in my heart," Bashag said. "The women in our village bear blighted fruit if they bear at all. Pray the Mother it will be different for Loronda. She is a widow who has had already enough sorrow. She has a child, a daughter named Tiu, who is a favorite of mine."

Marwen followed Bashag gingerly across a woven bridge and onto another and another. Her balance was off with the egg in her arms, and the bridges swayed under her feet. She found that the best way to cross them was quickly and without looking down. Women performing their labors in the moonlight, washing spidersilk and grinding grain for bread, bowed as they passed. Warm golden light like latesummer sun poured out of their windows and onto their dark faces.

Marwen could hear the woman's groans before they reached her home. Not the moans of discomfort, but the teeth-grinding fear-peaked sighs that come from deep pain.

A young woman was already at the inkle loom. Marwen was at once enchanted, for the girl was beautiful.

"Your counsel to me to ask the Mother to send the wizard's heir was good counsel, Lamia," Bashag said. "She is here to help us." Bashag turned to a child standing near Loronda. "Run away Tiu. I am here to care for your mother now. Poor thing. She was young enough to see the Taker when the old one came for her father. The little girl stared at Marwen for a moment with huge solemn eyes and then walked slowly toward the door. Lamia turned to Marwen.

"Marwen of Marmawell," the apprentice said as if she had known Marwen a long time, and then she smiled. Her skin was dark and silky. Her eyes were long and green as leaves. Her hair was shorn as a woman married or shamed, though Marwen was charmed by it, and her lips were a bright blood red.

Marwen smiled and turned toward the woman in childbirth when the horror of her dream in the sleeping winds returned to her. She swayed slightly on her feet. Somewhere in the room Bashag was busy with her preparations for Loronda Toymaker. Other women moved around the room, silent shadows bearing pots of steaming water and newly made spidersilk and hot white knives and thin needles. But Marwen's eyes were drawn again to the dark sleek apprentice.

Lamia was looking at her, and Marwen started. She felt awkward and ashamed. Lamia smiled, an exquisite, lovely, mysterious smile. In a single fluid movement, she cast her black cloak from off her bare shoulders and turned back to the inkle loom. "I was told you were beautiful," Marwen said.

Marwen shook her head as if she were plagued by thinwings. The spell roared in her ears like a fanned fire. Lamia had positioned the tension pegs and anchored the leash. Marwen took comfort in the familiar proceedings of the tapestry making, watched as the girl wound the same journey, missing the top peg, again, again, until the first warp was made. Her skills were excellent. The muscles in her bare brown arms rippled as she wound the warp and induced the trance by which she would tell the life of the child, speak its destiny in thread, weave the symbols of its future until the tapestry or the birth of the baby was complete.

"You have been taught by the best teacher," Marwen said.

"I was," she answered in her husky voice.

Marwen felt the earth tipping and turning beneath her. She recalled Grondil's favorite remedy for sickness: cure another. She turned toward the laboring woman. Loronda held herself rigidly still but for her chest that moved with shallow breaths. Her face was slick with sweat and her skin pale.

"How is it with you now, Loronda?" Bashag was asking.

The woman shook her head slightly. "This child comes fighting," she said quietly, almost without breath, and she smiled briefly.

Bashag lifted the red and purple silken drapes that covered the woman's body. "Not long, Loronda, not long," she said, but Marwen thought she heard a tremor in Bashag's voice. They began the long wait and watch as the woman suffered. Marwen had attended a few birthings, and at each one she had felt a tidiness of mind overcome her as her stored up dreams and passions and plans grew or shrank or were discarded in the revelation of this creation. But this time the spell on her heart loomed larger than the birthing. She forced herself not to think of the spell, and slowly, under the rhythmic chants of Bashag and the steady breathings of Loronda, Marwen was able at last to ease its effects. After a time she whispered, "Joy, Loronda, joy."

At that moment the laboring woman screamed through gritted teeth. The attending women's robes fluttered like bright flags in the wind. The spell shook Marwen like a hearth-cat shakes a fish.

"What is it, Marwen?" the young apprentice asked. "You look unwell."

Marwen straightened her shoulders. "This magic of a woman's journey to the borders of death ... to bring by the hand ... a soul into mortality, is powerful magic."

"A messy business," Lamia said, "one the hillgoats do without ceremony and by journeying no farther than the next field."

Marwen marveled that the girl could talk and do her trance at the same time. Then she turned to look into Loronda's face. Her eyes were closed. The women were kneeling around her, and their hands were on her abdomen, warm and comforting. Bashag was chanting a long hypnotic song of ease and relief.

Just then Marwen saw Lamia lift a free hand and, in a movement like a dancer's, twist it and bring it down. Loronda writhed and screamed in pain.

Marwen stood gaping. The other women in the room fluttered again, and Bashag renewed her chanting, but no one saw as once again Lamia, with a twist and plunge of her hand, made Loronda gasp and clutch at Bashag and throw her eyes open wide in disbelief. Lamia turned to Marwen with composed red lips.

Marwen felt as if she were in a dark dream.

"You are doing this," Marwen said.

Again the quick movement of Lamia's hand.

Again Loronda screamed.

"Mother help us," Bashag murmured.

"It is your apprentice," Marwen said. Bashag did not hear. Marwen felt chilled as if by a cold wind. "Stop her! She does not serve the One Mother."

Bashag glanced at her as if she were babbling in another language. Lamia looked at Marwen with surprise in her leaf-long eyes. "You are strong," she said, "stronger than I thought. What, do you not love me?"

Marwen felt her spine soften and her knees bend. "Yes, I love you," she thought. She said, "Why are you hurting her?"

"I merely speed her labor. You and I must be going, and quickly. Besides, I tire of it."

Bashag waved her hand in annoyance at Marwen.

"If there is nothing you can do but annoy Lamia, stand back," the old woman said to Marwen. Her lip was pouted out, dark and dry.

"But—but she does not serve the One Mother," Marwen said to Bashag. Bashag bent down to speak into Loronda's ear, little spells to relieve pain.

"Can no one hear me?" Marwen cried aloud.

"No, they cannot hear you," Lamia said. Her voice was deep and husky, her teeth white and even. "They are under an enchantment wherein they love me. They will not hear you if you tell them, for I have touched the prism moon."

Marwen stared and Lamia laughed, throwing her head back.

Prism moon ... prism moon ...

Words so old and sacred, Marwen seemed to have heard the words "prism moon" before, not with her own ears, but with the ears of that vast shared knowing of the One Mother.

Prism moon ...

She remembered once Grondil making a wish on the "close moon," and she remembered now the rest of the proverb Torbil had repeated: "All women are beautiful in winterdark, in part because of moonlit dark, in truth because of the unseen moon."

Marwen walked dreamlike to Bashag's side and put a hand on her shoulder.

"Bashag, tell me of the prism moon."

They filled her brain full, those words that whispered in her ears: prism moon.

No one heard her say louder, "Bashag!"

"I can hear you," a voice said at her side. A little girl, Tiu it was, Loronda's daughter, gazed up at her. "My mother is going to have a baby. Can you stop her from hurting my mother?"

She lifted her arm and pointed at Lamia. She was calm and unafraid.

"Go and play, little girl," Lamia said, and all the time her fingers worked the inkle loom with expert magic.

"No," Tiu said. "You are a witch."

"Go and play with your friends," Lamia said, deeply, almost kindly, but Marwen could hear the magic in her voice.

Tiu turned reluctantly, spellbound, and walked out of the

house. She was thin, her feet dainty, her hands delicate, but Marwen saw that her back was straight and strong. "She is right," Marwen said. "You are a witch."

"Bashag," Lamia called, and the Oldwife looked up. "This one troubles me and disturbs my trance. Can you not silence her?"

Bashag looked crossly at Marwen and gestured her to come away from Lamia.

Marwen chewed the inside of her cheek spasmodically and forced herself to resist using magic. Magic done in winterdark was doomed to have disastrous consequences. One spell in winterdark could disqualify her from receiving her staff. She tasted blood in her mouth. Slowly, deliberately, Lamia again lifted her arm, carefully brought it down with a strong graceful twist.

Loronda screamed. Before she had done screaming, Marwen ran to Lamia's side and pushed her hard, away from the inkle loom.

The girl landed on her side and was on her feet in a moment, springing and hissing like a stung hearthcat, her teeth and claws bared. She raised her arm in spellcraft.

"She is too young. This is too much for her. Wizard's heir or not, take her out." All the women were babbling at once, and instantly a dozen hands were on Marwen shushing her and pushing her out the door, their bright colored robes shimmering as banners in the wind.

CHAPTER FIVE

Do not be fooled. The storyspell, while it may be
spoken by anyone, and while it may be spoken in
winterdark, is one of the most difficult and powerful of spells: difficult because it cannot be
invoked by rote words, but only by the showing of
the soul; powerful because it can make a prince
of a poor man, a dragon of a child, a warrior of a
boy—forever. –*TENETS OF THE TAPESTRY*

ARWEN SHIVERED IN THE LIGHT OF
seven crescent moons. Behind Loron-
da's house, on the wide breast of the hill, a group of children
ran and played and made shrill whistles out of the tough stems
of three-wind woodies, flowers that blossomed under the night
sky. They jumped as if they could touch the moons, and
danced and raced with their hands outstretched as if there were
strings on the moons, and they could make them follow wher-
ever they willed. Behind Marwen, in the house, Loronda
screamed again, and Marwen moved away unsteadily. The children's laughter from the slope of the hill sounded like music in
her ears, and she moved toward them, making herself walk
instead of run, forcing herself to be calm, idling, and soothing
like a child with the magic in her.

Tiu was there, apart from the others. She was walking slowly around the single wingwand on the hill, the great black wing-wand with yellow markings. The children stopped their playing and stared as Marwen approached.

She smiled and nodded at Tiu, who stood a distance away. "Why are you not playing with the others?" she asked. She was amazed that Tiu had been able to resist Lamia's magic and had disobeyed the command to play. The little girl looked at the other children, and then Marwen understood. Marwen remembered herself alone on the slopes as a child, hovering outside a circle of children who laughed and whispered in a game that she was never allowed to join. In every little boy's face, she saw Maug, whose taunting and cruel tricks eventually became between them a sort of bond. It seemed so long ago, yet it had been only last summersun that she had left him in the wilderness between Kebblewok and Loobhan, on his way to the Oldest, to see to the remaking of his tapestry. She walked closer to the girl.

"Come, Tiu," Marwen said, holding her hand out to the little girl and hunkering down. The child approached and glanced at the others, who were closing around her in a circle. Marwen thought she heard, faintly and far away, a woman's scream, and she winced. The little girl seemed not to have heard, so Marwen smiled and steadied her voice.

"Do you know who I am?" Marwen asked.

"Yes," said Tiu soberly. "You are the wizard who changes herself into a white wingwand and flies about the night sky, and who keeps dragon treasure."

"So that is what they think," Marwen said. "But I am not a wizard yet, Tiu, for I do not have my staff."

"Can you grant wishes?" Tiu asked.

"What wish, Tiu?"

Marwen heard the children behind Tiu draw in a breath and then let it out in wild unintelligible whispers like a flock of callobirds.

"Mama says not even you could grant my biggest wish," Tiu answered when they were silent, "not unless, perhaps, you had your staff." She said it so softly that the others could not hear, and they crept closer.

"But my mother said she would be happy if there were snow, for then she could sell her sleds. I would wish for snow."

Marwen sat on the dry grass and plucked some three-wind woodies. The children sat around her, silently. More to comfort herself than Tiu, more to fill up her ears with her own voice than with the faint screams of Loronda, she invoked the storyspell with all her art.

"Norwind blows every day, but snow comes rarely to Ve. When norwind does bring snow, it whistles. Except in the mountains, perhaps but once at the height of winterdark will the norwind whistle through the hills and leave its gift of clean cold and snow. But have you ever heard of how the norwind got its whistle?" The children shook their heads slowly. Marwen smiled, for she could see that the children were already caught up in the storyspell. Marwen's hands continued to work deftly on the whistle.

"There was a time not long ago," Marwen continued in her spellsong voice, "when the snow did not fall for many years, and the children had grown up having never ridden the slopes, for the norwind had ceased to blow! The people missed the norwind terribly for other reasons too. 'How can we tell when it is time to bring in the laundry or start the bread to baking,' said the women to each other, and their meals were always late. As for the men, they stayed at work in the fields and shops long past the proper time, and they came home barking and frowning with sore backs. Everyone was in a bad mood, so of course no one ever bought toys, and the Mistress Toymaker and her children grew very hungry."

The children around Marwen lay down on the damp grass,

propped up on elbows, and in their eyes Marwen saw the hunger her voice spoke into their bellies. Only Tiu remained sitting up, her eyes flitting from Marwen's face to the whistle she fashioned while she spoke. Encouraged, Marwen strengthened the storytrance fiercely.

"The children of the Toymaker, a boy and a girl, went to ask advice of a magician who lived nearby. This magician was the second son of a wizard and was a great braggart, for he claimed to be able to understand the language of the winds.

"'Why does the norwind not blow?' the children asked him. 'Why does it not bring us snow?'

"'All I know is that the norwind won't blow this year, nor the next, nor the year after that,' said the magician. 'If you want to know why, go ask him yourself,' and then he laughed at them.

"The toymaker's children were particularly brave and skilled at flying wingwands, and so they journeyed to the shores of the northwest sea, from which the norwind blew, and climbed a high mountain to speak to the norwind, calling to him once, twice, three times. There was no answer, for in those days the norwind blew silently. But a callobird flew overhead and alighted on a huge hollow log."

Marwen continued to fashion the whistle while she spoke. Tiu put her hand on Marwen's.

"What is a log?" she asked.

Marwen's eyes shone. Tiu seemed to be the only one not under the storyspell. Marwen held up the hollow stem of the woodie. "Imagine a plant hundreds of times bigger than this. That is a tree, and a hollow log is the skeleton of a dead tree."

The children, who had listened with soberness to her tale so far, snickered in disbelief. Marwen continued.

"The callobird spoke to the children: 'The norwind cannot answer, for he has no voice, but even if he could, why should he? What have any of you done for the norwind except to curse him for his coldness?'

"The children had no answer for the callobird, but they refused to leave until they had spoken to the norwind. Fortunately, the boy and girl were clever and had remembered to bring with them tools that they had learned to use from their mother. They worked together and pushed another log into the hollow log. They cut a hole in the top, and when they were done, they had created a giant whistle.

"'Come, norwind,' they called. 'Come and see what we give you in return for your snow.'

"The norwind blew its icy silent self past them, biting their chins and frosting their eyelashes. But as he blew past them, he also blew past their whistle, and a long moaning cry filled the air. At first the wind shivered in disbelief. It blew again, a thin cold trill, and then again, and again.

"'See,' cried the children, 'we have given you a voice. Now will you come and bring snow to our village?' The wind picked them up with his invisible hand and put them on their wingwands. It blew their wingwands back to their village so fast that the wingwands scarcely had to beat their wings once. The norwind brought the villages snow that year, howling and wailing with fierce joy. The Mistress Toymaker became rich that winter selling sleds, and never again did the norwind cease to blow."

Marwen held out the whistle to Tiu. The children sat stupefied in the grass, unmoving, but Tiu's hand darted out to hold the toy.

"There is magic in this whistle," she said.

Marwen asked, "How so?"

"If I blow upon this whistle when norwind is nigh, it will bring snow."

Marwen said uneasily, "It is just a toy."

Tiu stood. She turned to run down the hill and then

stopped. When she looked at Marwen again, her face was pale and cold as starlight.

"Will you help my mother?" she asked.

"It will be over soon. She will be well again," Marwen said, too sorry for the little girl to be ashamed of her lie.

Tiu looked at her whistle and smiled. "If you say it, I know it will come true."

The girl scrambled down the dusk-drawn hill, disappearing into the seasonable gloom and the grasses like grey fur. The other children sat still before her, their eyes fixed and glazed. She raised her hand to break the spell, pleased that she had done so well, but she was pleased too soon. Before she uttered a word, the children's eyes snapped out of dreams, and their mouths snapped shut. They drew the backs of their hand across their mouths, and their eyes were dark slits. Marwen lowered her hand as they crept away into the darkness.

She shrugged and lifted a small rock. She looked at it for a long time, trying to think of its name, and then she dropped it. She looked up at the seven moons of Ve and at the stars. The bright constant star, Jersha, seemed strangely out of place. Marwen lowered her head, slowly picked up the small rock, then lifted her head again toward the stars. It was an illusion, she told herself, a trick of the eye because of the slope of the hill. The wind moaned in her ears, and she passed a hand over her eyes. She looked again. It was no illusion. The stars, familiar and beautiful, were all together slightly atilt, not in their proper place. And in the south were new stars she had never seen before.

"Great Mother," she whispered, "what is it?" She stood up. "What is it?"

Marwen heard once again, louder now, the screams of Loronda, rhythmic, steady. Marwen looked up at the sky in the wild hope that Camlach flew there looking for her, but the night sky was empty, changed, and in the north a wall of black cloud moved quickly, blotting out the stars.

She stood on her toes and called into the wind, "I'm not afraid! I'm not...." But she had the sensation that she had awakened a giant, for the moons looked down on her with lidded eyes, and the stars reached their arms to point at her, and the whole earth seemed to hold her up to their gaze. Even the sound of her own voice frightened her, for the wind snatched at it and blew it away over the hills. She had been wrong to tarry here, wrong to delay seeking the Staffmaker. She would get Zephrelle's egg from Loronda's house and slip away. Now. She rose and walked down the hill, stumbling on rocks she could no longer call by name.

CHAPTER SIX

Every selfless deed changes the destiny of the earth. *—TENETS OF THE TAPESTRY*

*T*HE ROBES OF THE ATTENDING WOMEN were limp and still, and between Loronda's cries was silence, but for the sound of Bashag mumbling to herself: "Not again, not again." The old woman paced, conferred with Lamia, then paced again. Marwen slipped in when the old woman's back was turned and picked up her wingwand egg.

When she was almost at the door, Bashag said, "Marwen." She stopped, but she did not turn around.

"Save the child," Bashag said to her. The old woman came to her, faced her, palms outstretched. "The child may be dying. Loronda will die. There is no Oldwife's power to save her, but perhaps ..."

Marwen stared at the old woman. A greyish film covered the inside of her bottom lip. Marwen could scarcely breathe in the presence of the young apprentice. It was as if her beauty was a perfume that had been applied to heavily.

"I am unnamed as a wizard," Marwen said, as if being named would change the taboo against winterdark magic.

"Please. My spells are spent into the waters in winterdark," Bashag said.

"Mine are forbidden," Marwen said. The old woman didn't answer. Her face had become slick, like oiled dough, and her bottom lip moved up and down.

Marwen remembered her promise to Tiu, "Your mother will be well again."

The law was for good reason. Every act of magic changed the world in small or big ways, and one who wielded such power must needs look far to see the end of her spellwork. In summersun one could look far, in winterdark, no.

"If you say it, I know it will come true," Tiu had answered.

Marwen looked at Lamia, sleek and strong before the loom, and she lay the egg down carefully. There was something good and powerful in choosing, even if one chose wrongly. And who could say this was wrongly chosen, to relieve a sister's pain, to give her life?

She willed the magic to come to her, and it came quickly and easily. She felt it explode in her chest, ripple to her feet and fingers. She placed her hand on Loronda's belly and felt it tense and quiver beneath her hand as she spoke the words for life and strength against evil. The smell of sour sweat and sweet blood filled Marwen's nostrils. She heard a sound like wet paper tearing and watched as Loronda's face became grey with moonlight, watched as her lips drew back from her teeth. Marwen grasped the woman's hand and spoke the words more loudly.

"The spell is working!" Bashag cried.

Marwen felt her own magic working against an equally

strong magic. She heard Lamia's breathing come more quickly. Marwen ground her teeth in concentration, felt her head throb with the effort. "Torlenthe, Loronda, torlenthe," she whispered.

In a moment Bashag's voice rang out. "The babe is born! It is a boy!" The attending women leaped up, sleeves and hems flapping and floating gaily.

Lamia's weaving slowed. Her shoulders slumped. Bashag busied herself with her ministrations to the baby and chatted joyfully as she did so. But Marwen heard with only one ear, saw with only one eye. Her consciousness was full of another reality, a truer reality that filled a larger world: the spell.

"Though you are unnamed, yet you have saved the child," Bashag said to Marwen softly, her toothless mouth lisping the words sweetly. Loronda, murmuring weakly, drifted to sleep.

But Marwen could not speak. The spell was heavy upon her now. It pulled at her, willed her to come, to follow. She looked at Bashag and saw not the child, not the crooning Oldwife, but only the blood and discarded flesh at Loronda's feet.

"I have heard it said that any magic done in winterdark is sorcery," Lamia said. Her voice was smooth and cold as ice. The moonlight passed pale over her face.

Marwen began to shiver uncontrollably. She had spent much magic in saving Loronda's life and the life of the baby. She had no strength now to resist the spell that weighed down on her with a bitter force. Her eyes burned, and her face flushed hot. The spell was so close upon her now that she could decipher it almost. Marwen knew that Lamia was not the source, but only the bearer of the spell, and that though her help for Loronda had strengthened the spell, it had weakened Lamia's power.

"Who is doing this to me?" Marwen asked.

Even when Marwen worked no spell, the magic was a powerful force around her, and a question she demanded was not easily ignored. Lamia's shoulders stiffened, and her mouth opened to answer, but no words came. She went slowly, silent as a shadow to the rushweed fire and drew from her tapestry pouch a small bag. With a graceful movement, she cast some powder from the bag into the fire. The powder blossomed into puffs of pink smoke above the flames, and Lamia breathed in the smoke with quiet concentration.

Marwen smelled the unmistakable scent of shordama, a powder used in love potions by Oldwives who dared to interfere with such things.

"You will harm the child," Marwen said, swallowing the bile in the back of her throat, but the scent was maddeningly sweet.

The girl shrugged. "I am addicted," she said. She threw another handful of powder onto the fire.

Marwen did not look to see if the other women had noticed the pink smoke hovering over their heads. She made a gesture with her hand to put out the fire and then stopped herself. Gathering her wits and strength, she took and emptied the water jar onto the fire. Again Lamia shrugged. She began licking the stuff off her fingers.

"Tell me who makes this spell on me and why?"

"Someone who knows you. The wizard's true heir ..." Lamia said, and then her mouth clamped shut, and her eyes narrowed.

Marwen gripped her tapestry pouch. "But I am the wizard's heir."

"Imposter!" Lamia hissed. "You know who the true heir should be. You left him to die once, left him without a wingwand in the wilderness because you knew. But with his magic he lived. He came to Shadrah the Oldest, to whom I was apprenticed, and she died calling him Wizard."

For a long time Marwen did not answer. She followed the

intricate stitching of her tapestry pouch with her forefinger, mindlessly following the maplike thread of the embroidery, patterned like the constellations of the stars. Inside it was her tapestry that she had crossed Ve for, the tapestry that she had battled a dragon for, that she had almost died for, the tapestry that told her she must seek her staff. And along the way she had left Maug, the sole survivor of her village, alone in the wilderness. Maug, her childhood tormentor, a boy her own age. She felt the black hand of the spell ease its hold on her heart. She laughed shortly.

"Maug? Maug is the one who places a spell on me? By what power?"

Marwen was aware that Bashag had shooed away all the other women and with them their glowfly crystals. Only two crystals remained, and the glowflies within them were sluggish and flitted about lazily. The light was dim. The dark-headed witch became a long shadow in the moonlight, a still shadow, barely breathing. She stopped sucking on her fingers.

"By what power? I have already told you," she said dreamily. "By the power of the prism moon."

The memory of the shadows and the stars and the eyes of the children returned, and the power of the spell clutched and squeezed again at Marwen's heart. It was as if she were hearing the words all over again for the first time. Surely this was the magic that had filled her moon dream, the magic that had darkened more deeply the winternight sky—the magic of the prism moon. Windsigh, temperate and gentle in summersun, blew a cold gust through the east window.

"Tell me of the prism moon," Marwen said softly.

Lamia leaned forward and said, "Come to Loobhan and see."

"Has Maug also placed this spell upon the babies of Wrea-then-Rills?"

Lamia pulled back into the shadows, the glint gone from her eyes, as if she thought Marwen an unworthy opponent.

"You do not know what a wizard should know. This happens not only in Wreathen-Rills, but in all Ve. Even the earth aborts her own and is barren. The upwellings here drown the fields of grain and elsewhere come not at all. The young people do not dance, and they forget how to play at love."

"All this because of the prism moon?"

Lamia's teeth flashed in the dim light; her hair around her eyes was like a glossy bit of black sky. "Shadrah had meant to use the power of the moon to reweave his tapestry, for you did not come. But she is dead. Now you are the only one who can make my master his tapestry so he can get his staff."

"Lamia, you were deceived. Maug is a trickster, one who has hated me since our childhood, though I cannot tell you why."

"I have seen his magic," she said, and her eyes looked far away as if she were remembering terrible things. "I have seen him vanish, all but his head floating, and this before he ever held the prism moon."

Marwen smiled at Lamia as if she had already persuaded her. "But of course. When we traveled together once, he took from an Oldwife named Politha a magical blanket that makes whatever it covers invisible. I saw it with my own eyes, and with it Maug deceives you into thinking that he has magic."

"Lies! He told me that you would lie. He told me also that I would find you here, that you would come this way to the mountains. But think of this Marwen: by the power of the prism moon he has cast a spell upon you. Can you not feel it? Only one born to the magic could wield such power."

Marwen stepped back as if to flee from the sound of the girl's voice, and then she was still. The air of premonition was in her nostrils, and in that moment's silence, she heard with her heart what, in the next, she heard with her ears.

Into the silence curled the thin wail of the baby's cry, and at the sound, Marwen felt the hair on her forearms prickle.

Bashag was holding the baby in her arms, looking intently at him. She frowned, and her bottom lip protruded, so it looked as if it were another appendage and not a lip at all.

"That is not right," she said shortly.

She examined the baby competently, wonderingly. For a long time she looked into the baby's eyes, watched its feeble movements beneath the blanket, touched its cheek. Finally, she put the baby down as if it weighed more than she could bear.

"The baby is not right," Bashag said. She walked to where Lamia sat and stood before her, her arms limp at her sides, her eyes half-closed.

"In its mind, it is not right. It does not want to suckle; it does not cry normally."

Lamia looked at Marwen narrowly; then a gleam came into her leaf-long eyes. The older woman pulled the child's tapestry from the inkle loom. Marwen could not help but look, though she knew what she would see. The entire tapestry was a twilight grey but for one symbol in the middle, the only symbol that had been woven in the tapestry: a round white moon.

"Begone, sorceress! This is your doing. It had been better if the child had died," Bashag said, and her voice was hard and full of terror. Then Marwen felt the flesh on her back quiver, for Bashag addressed not Lamia, but herself. Marwen tried to speak, but the baby had begun to cry, a pitiful mournful wail that filled her ears and silenced her. How had she thought that she was free to break the Tenets against winter spellcraft? How far could she see in the crisscross shadows of moondrift?

In that moment when she was not free to speak, Marwen knew that she was not free at all, but bound by the cords of a great spell. And at the end of her cords waited someone who hated her: Maug.

Maug it was who had grown up with her, who had begged to be allowed to follow her into the wilderness after the burning of Marmawell. Now it was no longer this Maug whom she had to deal with, but a more powerful Maug, who somehow had enchanted Shadrah the Oldest and now was called Master by Lamia, her apprentice. Perhaps she had always known that within him he carried the seeds of power. Certainly, she had feared him all these months, had borne like a disease her promise to him to be witness at his tapestry making. Now the shadow in her heart had a name, and it pulled at her, pulled her backward by the hair.

Marwen did not look at Bashag or Lamia. She knelt by the woman Loronda until the new mother opened her eyes and stirred.

Marwen held her hand.

"I am still unnamed," Marwen said. "But when I have my staff, and when it is sunrise, I will try to help you."

At that she picked up Zephrelle's egg and walked to the door. She could feel Bashag's eyes upon her, feel her hope draining like the blood from her face.

"Stop!" Lamia cried, and the magic in the command caused Marwen to hesitate. She placed her left foot before her right. Then her right before her left, easier this time. The next step was easier still. "Stop!" Lamia commanded again, her voice full of authority and magic. In her mind Marwen saw herself turning around, stepping back into the house; she felt herself giving in to the spell, imagined the relief of falling into the dark and quiet.... She forced herself to take one more step. Immediately, the spellhold eased.

"Where is she going?" she heard Lamia say to Bashag, and then more forcefully, "Where is she going?" But Marwen did not stop. She crossed the bridges, walked past the women who cooked over bubbling hot springs, past the men who collected the spidersilk larvae into bowls, and into the dark night and the mists like fallen cloud.

As she walked toward the towering mountains, Marwen thought she heard the plaintive tune of a three-wind woodie whistling over the marshlands of Wreathen-Rills. Norwind began to blow, and with it came a driving snow.

CHAPTER SEVEN

The staff cannot be given,
Nor bought by tears or gold.
The gift is rightly hidden
In the reaches of the soul.
—A LOST SONG, REMEMBERED
FROM HER APPRENTICESHIP BY
BASHAG OLDEST

*B*EYOND THE VILLAGE THE GROUND began to swell and become drier and firmer. Marwen aimed to go through a high valley between the first mountains. The snow blew into her face and clung to her cloak that she had wrapped around herself and Zephrelle's egg.

When she had walked for an entire wind, the slope began to steepen and the egg to feel like the weight of gold. She sat to rest on the wet snow. She was alone in the darkness, she was sure, but looked about in fear that someone had followed her. Maug's spell dogged her steps.

Marwen folded her arms on her knees and rested her head there. She had no idea where she was. She had never been completely sure of where Mt. Ornu was, but on Torbil's maps it had not seemed like finding a mountain was so difficult a thing. She imagined Torbil there beside her now, gruff and breathing great clouds of warm air into the cold.

"What, did your magic not take care of you?" he would tease. "Did a mountain scare away one who has frightened dragons?" Not a mountain, but a girl named Lamia and a boy named Maug, she would say. "A very big girl? A very big boy?" Torbil would answer in return. But she wouldn't mind. She would bear his teasing and laugh and love him. And then too there was Camlach. But at the thought of him, instead of warm stirrings in her belly, there was heat like a pain. A sensation of drowsiness filled her. "I will sleep," she thought, "and then I will return to Torbil and beg Camlach to help me."

But in the next moment, she was on her feet, her heart slamming in her chest, her muscles tensed, her head turned toward the sky. The darkness seemed awash with a grey light. Flying overhead was a great black wingwand with yellow markings upon its wings.

Marwen crouched low. She held her breath and buried her hands into the snow and soil as if she could disappear into the darkness. She swallowed hard. There was the faint odor of shordama on the wind. The black wingwand eclipsing the stars circled once further uphill and then charted westward to disappear behind the mountain. The snow thickened, and the stars were blotted out by the swift-blowing clouds. Marwen smiled grimly. The snow she had made for Tiu could kill her in these mountains before she found the Staffmaker, but it had hidden her from Lamia.

"The One Mother is merciful," she whispered. She pulled her cloak tightly around her. The blue-black sky was filled with moons like half-closed eyes. She tried to relax. The muscles in her whole body were taut as loom threads.

Marwen touched the smooth round egg. It was warm with life. The falling snow reflected on its surface like a snowglass that she had shaken as a child, when she had watched the snow fall through the water onto the little clay trees and carven weedsheep at the bottom of the glass. It was like the vision that she'd had in the spring near Kebblewok.

"Mother of magic, do you see me?" Marwen whispered to the egg. "I have not known what a wizard should know. I have been lovesick for a prince and heartsick for a staff, and now I am spellsick. I promised Maug that I would reweave his tapestry for him at the first chance. I broke my promise, and now because of my wickedness, he wields the prism moon. Forgive me now and help me. Have I not read the books? What is this prism moon?"

The reflected light curved on the round surface of the egg, and in it she could see a book with pages that fluttered in the wind, with words that glinted singly like stars. Marwen stared at the vision in the egg a moment. Then quickly she took from her tapestry pouch the journal of her father, plainly bound, with pages of thin paper that whispered as the sounds of the dead when she touched them.

The words were dark in the moonlight, and so between Marwen's cupped hands, she formed the bright werelight that had been the gift that came with her Oldwife naming. It required no spell to make it, and so it was safe to use in winterdark. In a moment it burned cool in her palm, and she balanced it lightly on one finger while she leafed carefully though the thin pages. There was still so much she had not read. Much of it was difficult to read, for Nimroth had formed his letters in a strange cursive style. Other parts of the book were written in runes, understandable only by magic and only when the words willed themselves to be read. These Marwen searched, for knowledge of the prism moon would be a knowledge for the higher orders. Once she stopped at a passage written so quickly that she could not read it at all, but for one sentence: "Love tears me two ways." Much later, when she understood what it meant, she tried to find that passage, but she was never able to find it again.

All during norwind and into the next, she read, bending her mind to the interpreting of words. Her little werelight flickered in the wind and the falling snow. Small trickles of perspiration ran down her back, partly from the warmth of her cloak, partly from the concentration it took to decipher the words and at the same time fend off the shadow of the spellsickness. When her head hurt so that she thought she could not read another word, the werelight flashed brightly over a page of anciently styled runes. Instantly, the words could be understood, becoming symbols of sound, naming that which was unnameable—prism moon.

"... the little moon that orbits, brilliant, spectral ..."

"... some say that in the mountains it hovers so close to the earth that one could ..."

"... love is the power of the prism moon—love and lust and fertility are the gifts she brings to earth ..."

"... inviting all and any to find it and touch it, and reap forever adoration to themselves, unending ..."

"... no one alive has found it ..."

"... a rhyme, a parable, a myth ..."

"... real, say those who have died seeking it ..."

Marwen read for a long time.

"The force that drags at me is not death or darkness, but love?" she said aloud. No, not love, but lust, she thought, and a lust wrongly held, a lust that longs to own and enslave. A dark magic.

She put the book back into its oilskin wrappings and gathered the egg into her arms. She had thought that knowing would ease her fear and the power of the spell, but it did not.

She held the egg up before her eyes. "How do you come to have visions in you, egg? Did all the magic I spoke around

Zephrelle soak into your shell?" She looked around her. The mountainside was cold and silent and dark. Perhaps even the One Mother could not see her here. "Little egg, if you are full of visions, show me my prince...."

The snow reflected more brightly in the egg, like stars, like winking eyes, like teeth, like tears, tears upon the face of a man, the face of a man in the egg.

"Camlach," Marwen said, and her voice whispered into the hills. She could see him, little in the egg. No, it was not Camlach, but someone marvelously like him—it might have been Camlach in five or nine years. His garb was royally made, princely dyed, but he hung from chains on a damp prison wall. Marwen knew that he was Ronor, Camlach's older brother. Facing him, his back to Marwen, a young man with blemishes on his neck was holding a light to the prince's face. It was a glorious light. No candle or crystal could have made it. Weakly, Ronor fought to be free. His chained hands strained at their bonds, his mouth slavered, and his eyes could see nothing but the light.

"Stop!" Marwen said aloud. "It would be better to kill him."

The light went out. The man fell limp against his chains. His eyes, still open, saw nothing at all.

Maug turned to her, his face filling the egg. "For you," his lips said without sound.

Marwen clutched the egg against her breast and would not look. After a time she stood and hefted the egg, cushioned it against her belly, felt the flutterings of life, and then walked in the direction that Lamia's wingwand had flown. Bashag must have told Lamia where to look for the Staffmaker. She glanced down at the egg and saw in it the movement of visions that she knew now would not stop. She would not see, she told herself. She would not look.

The smooth snowy thighs of the mountain slope later gave way to drier rocky shoulders and steep narrow necks. Pebbles slid beneath her feet and echoed in the hills around. She could hear her own breath, loud and labored, as if there were not enough air.

The mountains rose in ascending heights, rock towering above rock, land dipping into small soft valleys and out again onto great dizzying bluffs and steep scarps that ended in dull dark peaks. Still the snow fell. Now it did not blow, but fell fat and white. She stayed to the riverbanks and passes. The river smoked in the cold, furring the bankpines with frost. She tried to see into its depths, but she saw no fish, no bubble of life. The pale light was absorbed by its dull surface.

Marwen walked for an entire cycle of winds. And then another. In that time she had gone down into a rocky valley and up onto the grassless face of a mountain whose top disappeared into the darkness. Behind her were the sparse stars; before her was only the blackness of an earth that rose against her. West and south she went, in the direction of the black wingwand.

She felt at times as if the world and the egg had traded places, that she walked inside the egg and held the world in her arms. The stars bent in the bubble-sided sky, and the moons stretched and squashed and were jokesters. The mountains turned their glossy convex visions inward to where she held the little world. She could not stop seeing faces in its sloshy oceans, faces of young women weeping and babies blind and Maug's face against the dark and the stars, blotting out the moons, turning, searching, listening, sniffing. He knew she sweat in the cold, knew she climbed and breathed like a bellows into the wind. He breathed for her. When he slept, she slept.

MARWEN AWOKE SHIVERING and confused. She did not

remember sheltering between two rocks to sleep. She could no longer tell which direction was west. The snow had stopped, but the stars were hidden completely by clouds, and the moons shone faintly as behind a veil. She ate some dried berries, hard as nuts, that she'd collected along the way. Her tooth slipped on one too smooth and bit her tongue. The blood was warm in her mouth, and she did not spit it out, but swallowed it.

Her sleep had strengthened her. She did not know where west was, but she could feel the nearness of the Master Staffmaker now. It was almost as cold and fearsome a magic as Lamia's, but it was also a magic of creation.

The half-hidden moons cast a blue light on the snow. There was no sound but the wind in her ears and the echo of breath in her lungs. The slope graded steeply. Soon, she knew, she would have to lay down the egg. Soon, but not now.

She found food among the rocks and rivers, winter berries, weed that crisped nicely over her werelight fires. But as the winds passed and the spell deepened, she found less and less food, and she began to chew ice and suck on snow-covered pebbles. Mountain grew into mountain. The whole world had become a crown of sheer cliffs, sharp ridges, and crags of snow-scrubbed rock. She lost track of windcycles and days, but she knew that she had been walking among the giants a very long time by the slow drift of the moons in the winternight sky.

She began to look for the Taker in the water-worn canyons and dry old riverbeds. The faces of the mountains had been worn into soft folds in places and bare slag-shedding cliffs in others. Nothing grew but brittle grasses, chafing together in the wind. And everywhere was silence, the wind, the sky, and the spoor of unseen animals. At times she forgot her staff and was haunted by the hallucinations of falling stars and moons the size of a man's heart.

And then she came to a mountain that rose into the sky

before her like the end of the world. It was beautiful and fear-some—and familiar. She lay the egg down. She recognized the mountain. Her chest was tight and sore. She drew her tapestry out of its pouch and unfolded it with shaking hands. She grasped it with two fists, unable to still their shaking, and held the tapestry close to her face like an old woman who could scarcely see. It was the same mountain that had been woven into her tapestry, she was sure.

"The Mother willing, this is the mountain I seek," she said aloud to assure herself that she was still alive, that this was not a vision.

She climbed. She was shivering again, but somehow she could not recall the words for heat and fire spells. She came to a sheer wall of rock and could go no further. The magic of the Staffmaker was up, higher on the mountain, but there was no pathway. With one hand she scrambled up onto a ledge and then onto another narrower ledge. Her breaths were coming in dry sobs. She could not carry the egg another moment, no not one. She held it before her eyes.

In it she saw Maug standing before a great gathering of people, and in his hand he held a beating heart. He laughed, a silent laugh that went on and on and on. Marwen looked into the face of his victim, a girl it was, her breast laid aside like a broken doll's, her eyes alive but filled with coming death—grey eyes—like her own—her very own, for the victim was herself.

With a great cry that started in her bowels, Marwen struck the egg against the sharp-ridged rock. The egg cracked and with it the vision.

A beastlike groan came out of her mouth. She was shaking violently, and she clenched her jaw to keep her teeth from clacking together.

"Zephrelle, forgive me," she whispered with lips like dried flowers. The fluid from the egg seeped warm over her hand. It

had been many winds since she had drunk anything but melted
snow. She lifted her hand to her mouth, touched the fluid to
her lips, and then, accidentally at first, tasted. It was warm and
sweet like mothers' milk. Her body trembled with instant pleasure. With all the strength that remained in her body, she
broke off a piece of the shell and scooped out the warm meat
of the egg. She ate until she was sated.

FOR A LONG time she sat very still, sure in her mind that
she would be ill. But her body became stronger within minutes, and her mind began to clear. She could remember the
spells for heat and fire, and she thought that she would not die.

The rock wall loomed as high as ever before. But now she
could see a path to her left, the width of a small foot. It wound
downward for a little while, widening, and then, perhaps, it
would climb again. And if it did not, she wondered if she
would care.

She continued her journey, feeling lighter now, her arms
blessedly, achingly empty, her mind full of nothing but forcing
her body to put one foot in front of the other. The wind whispered in her ears like the twittering of a wingwand. After a
long time the path turned upward again, around the massive
wall of rock and into trees.

She had seen only one tree in her life. Now before her was a
herd of them, mammoth needle-lofted trees with tough-
skinned stems, that rose before her like lords of the mountain.
They danced only with their arms and together sang a song
that frightened Marwen with its beauty. Once she had been to
the ocean. It sounded like the ocean—a sea of thin leaves,
waves in the wind.

Beyond the trees was a sloping meadow covered in snow,
and beyond the expanse of snow, points of light shone like
lanterns in huts, gleaming through east windows.

The dark seemed deeper now that light was ahead. Marwen stumbled toward the lights, through the grove of trees into the field of snow. The snow was deep, almost up to her knees, but she could not feel the cold anymore, though her cloak was heavy with ice.

She stopped. From somewhere she could hear music. Snowflakes dusted down, and the wind looped them up and away, driving them into soft white drifts.

The snow around her legs felt warm, and she was drowsy.

"I will sleep here," she thought, "just for a little while." Her eyes would not stay open any longer. She lay down and dreamed.

CHAPTER EIGHT

A new moon, and my soul was dark. A new love,
and my soul is light and my eye sees.
—NOTES OF NIMROTH, FROM A LATER JOURNAL

S HE THOUGHT SHE WAS LYING IN A pool of warm sunlight, the dust motes floating silently in the air above her. But the dust motes were phantoms behind her eyes, and the warmth was from a fire. This she realized as she became more fully awake. Windbells were ringing somewhere nearby.

She opened her eyes, but she did not move.

Whatever this place was, it protected her from the full strength of Maug's spell. She breathed deeply. Directly above her, in rows along the rafters, hung nets of roots and vegetables and cheeses, pungent smelling, earth smelling. Beside her was a small pile of wood, thin sticks of it, and long, about as long as she was tall. It too had a maddening earth scent not of rotting or degeneration, but of something transforming, ripening, becoming purer and stronger. Marwen reached out to touch a piece of the wood. It was smooth as spidersilk but strong, and Marwen sensed magic coming from the wood or from somewhere in the room.

She sat up.

Carefully she picked up one of the sticks. It was heavy in her hand, like lead, and yet her hand delighted in the weight of it, as a mother does in the weight of her baby in her arms or as a musician does in the weight of the cupplehorn.

A voice behind her startled Marwen.

"What, did no one ever teach ye any manners? Put that down. What will the Master Staffmaker say? Put it down, I say."

He was old, very old, his skin wrinkled in every direction like crumpled paper, and between the wrinkles were blotches and moles and pox scars. He was hunched beneath his rough-woven robe like the trunk of a tree bent in the wind, and his bones were wide and thick as old branches, as if his frail body had once been powerful. His eyes betrayed a strong and clever mind trapped inside a body that was half a heartbeat away from death. Marwen wondered for a moment, wickedly, if this old man was the Taker's husband.

"Master Staffmaker?" Marwen said, obeying the old man's command. "Do you know the Master Staffmaker?"

The old man drew away from her. His legs were bowed and brown beneath his tunic as the unearthed roots of a tree.

"I might. I might. Why d'ye ask? And who is it that asks it?"

"I am Marwen of Marmawell, and I have come this long way to ask an important favor of the Master Staffmaker."

The old man coughed a dry laugh and stumped away.

"Favors? Favors? The skin-flinted old bark don't do anyone favors." He stopped suddenly and looked at her sideways. "What d'ye want?"

"I have come for my staff. I am the wizard's heir," she said. She almost laughed in relief. She had made it to the mountain home of the Staffmaker, and alone. How she would remind Torbil again and again.

He came closer and peered at her. She could hear the bones in his jaw creaking. The old man snorted, "You? You're a girl."

Marwen lifted her chin. "That one your age should notice," she said.

The old man spluttered and moved his mouth faster. "Ya randy cheek. Out into the snow with ye. Out I say!"

Marwen frowned and did not move. "Your discourtesy deserved mine. Will you not tell me where I might find the Master Staffmaker?"

"I know him well, but those who are worthy to see him usually find him without my help. You I would na tell anyways. The other lass, she was kind to me, sweet and most mannerly, a lovely lass...."

Marwen jumped to her feet. "Lamia? You told her where to find the Staffmaker?"

"No, I did na say that. I said she was respectful." The old man, confident now that he had the upper hand, sat smugly on the greatrug, his back to Marwen.

"You mustn't tell her. What is your name?"

"Name is Bim," he said.

"Bim, sir, you must not tell her. She wants to keep me from getting my staff. She says her master is heir, and her master is Maug, who fools people with a magical blanket into believing he has powers, and ..."

"Ach, stop. Your tale is as long and gormless as the other's. Begone." He gestured her away.

Marwen said nothing for a moment. She didn't want to go—she felt safe here. This man was obviously a servant of the Staffmaker, and so the Staffmaker must be nearby at least.

"Well," she said, "then I must thank you for helping me. I might have died in that snow. How did you find me?"

"Heard the Taker's music," he said without turning to her. "Figured if it were for me she'd come, I'd chase the old dame off 'fore she got to me, but it were for you. I brought you in thinking if she got you she might remember ol' Bim. I hate it when people die outside my door...." He stopped.

The old man's back was as stiff as a tree. She looked at the sticks on the floor by the hearth, and she felt the magic in the room again.

"Bim," she said, testing the idea that had come into her mind, "you grow overbold from long years service to too lenient a master. Go tell the Staffmaker I am come."

The old man twisted his crooked body to face her.

"I am no servant, you young ..." His mouth fell open, and his eyes bulged, realizing his mistake. Instantly, the countenance of the man changed to one not of a servant, but of a man of old, old magic.

"The other one could not guess," he said.

"The other one borrows her magic," Marwen answered. She was not pleased with her trick. As a child the wizard was, in her mind, a protector, a vessel of wisdom and knowledge, the final benefactor, and dwelling beside the wizard was the legendary Staffmaker. Now she was the wizard's heir, and before her sat the Staffmaker, who was, after all, a mortal man. She fought off an urge to laugh and a wrenching feeling of fear as if she were falling.

"Please, listen to me," she said.

But Bim shook his head. "You are the second who comes to me," he said. "Both of you demand, but you show me no sign. You bring me nothing from my dreams. I am old and tired. All that I have loved is dead, my life fires are spent, and still the Mother does not send me what I desire most."

But Marwen was not listening to the sorrows of the old man. She could smell the spell in the wind that seeped in under the door, and she knew that without the staff of the wizard, she would be overcome by it.

"My father was Nimroth," she said.

"So says the other of her master. That is a name with no magic in this house," the Staffmaker said.

Marwen forced her shoulders and neck to stiffen.

"I have a sign." She fumbled at her tapestry pouch and gently pulled out her tapestry, wrapped carefully in oilcloth. She placed it in his hands. He eyed her with a yellowed warty eye, and then, with fingers like the twigs of a tree, lifted the corner. He pushed the tapestry away.

"No," Marwen said. "My calling was not placed there, but here, along the top, as a border. She unrolled the tapestry—not too much, for it is unseemly to do so. The old man did not look.

His yellowed eyes were closed, and his withered chest was utterly still as if no breath entered him. Marwen too stopped breathing and then started when the old man finally spoke.

"I need not look. I feel the magic on you, but you bring me nothing of my dreams. The other who came, she too was full of magic, powerful magic, and she says she is merely the servant of the true wizard."

"It is the magic of the prism moon that you felt," Marwen said.

The old man's jaw began to creak and quiver. He stood up slowly, quaking like a leafless tree in the wind.

"Maug has stolen it," Marwen said simply.

"The lady love? The prism moon?" He spoke as if in a trance or in disbelief. A toothless smile trembled on his lips, and then he frowned fiercely and hunched his old shoulders. Once, Marwen thought, he would have looked proud and brave. "It is not wise to taunt the Staffmaker. I have a magic of my own...."

"I do not taunt you, Master Staffmaker. With the prism moon a boy named Maug has cast a spell upon me."

For the first time the old man looked directly into her eyes, and after he had looked for a time, he nodded slightly. "You do have the look of Nimroth about you."

Marwen knelt on one knee. "Sire, the stars are changed, and the wind weeps with the sound of babies crying. Who can heal the earth but the wizard?" Again the old man nodded. "I am young, but is it not said that the One Mother gives strength to those whom she calls? Please, sire, will you make for me my staff and give me my naming?"

But before he could answer, a scream was heard from without.

Marwen and Bim ran out of doors where two figures struggled in the snow. She recognized the girl first by her voice: Lamia.

She was cursing and squealing and sputtering out half-formed spells, while a man was clamping his hand over her mouth and getting bitten for his efforts. In a swift movement, the girl broke away. In her hand was a knife that glinted in the moonlight like a thin mirror, a sliver of glass. Lamia struck out at the other, but Marwen blocked her arm, and the stab of the witchling was too weak to hurt him. In that moment of advantage, he gained control of Lamia, knocking her knife into the snow.

Bim held up a blazing torch.

"By the Mother! What is this?"

The man spoke from beneath his winter hood. "I come here seeking Marwen, daughter of Nimroth. The villagers pointed me here, but as I came to the east window, I found this girl, her knife poised and both of you inside, unknowing."

He eased his hold on her, and Lamia tore away. She stumbled and fell panting into the snow.

"I told you to stay with the Oldwife up the hill," Bim said to Lamia.

"Then you know her?" the young man said. Lamia was on her feet again, stamping and cursing as she brushed the snow from herself. Marwen moved closer to the young man. She knew his voice. She took the torch and held it before his narrow face. The flame danced in the wind.

"Camlach!" she cried, and she dropped the torch at his feet.

He laughed and grasped both her hands. "You always find me in trouble and come to my rescue."

She too laughed and threw her arms around his neck, and he picked her up and swung her around. Then he was saying her name and crushing her to his chest, squeezing the breath out of her, and she felt as light as the wingscale of a newborn wingwand. Though the wind and cold had burned the skin on her face brown and dry, yet in that moment she knew she was beautiful.

"You must not love her, but only me," Lamia said.

Camlach broke from their embrace to look at the girl in the snow. In the half-light a look of confusion passed over his face. Then he laughed, a sound of surprise, delight, as one laughs at the tricks of a magician, not bewitched, but interested, piqued, startled. Then he turned to Marwen, his eyes full of the torchlight that burned in the snow at his feet. "I am already enchanted by another," he said.

But Marwen had remembered. "How long it took you to come to me," she said to him.

"You sent me away," he said gently, "and then ..."

"You promised to help me in the staffseeking," she said, stepping back.

"I am here," he answered.

Lamia lunged at the Staffmaker. She shook him.

Camlach stepped up to separate them, but Lamia let go.

"I told the Oldwife to keep you," Bim said, cowering.

"Did you think that the spells of a village Oldwife could

hold me, old man? I was the apprentice to the Oldest, and now I am emissary to the wizard's heir. Give me a staff for him, for I know now you are no servant, but the Staffmaker himself."

He stood a moment, then doddered into the house. "Lovely lass. Clever too," Bim mumbled to himself. He stopped in the doorway and looked about him as if he were just waking up.

With Camlach beside her, Marwen felt brave and bold.

"She has touched the prism moon, Bim Staffmaker. Do not forget," she said.

"Outside the window, you say? With a knife? The good magic comes not with knives, now, does it. I am old. Where's my apprentice? No, no apprentice. Prism moon, eh? But she don't bring it. They both don't bring the gift—neither girl brings it. Girls! Ah, Nimroth, what've ye done? The one's a lovely clever lass though...."

"If only Bashag could see this," Marwen said to Lamia when Bim was in the house. Her voice was sharp and unafraid.

Lamia laughed cruelly. "Bashag will never see anything again. I have made her eyes as blind as her heart. She seemed to think, as you do, that she could teach me anything." She looked at Marwen and at Camlach as if measuring their combined strength. Scowling, she whirled around in a billow of black robes and seemed to dissolve into the night.

CHAPTER NINE

Callobird, sing for me,
Sing your starlight song.
Dance for me your nest-love dance
All the winter long.
—A VEAN CHILD'S NURSERY RHYME

ARWEN LOOKED AWAY FROM CAM-
lach's gaze and toward his cloak that lay
steaming in golden folds by the door. The sheep cheese and
bread that Bim had lain before them remained uneaten. The
prince listened as she told him of all that had befallen her since
they had parted, beginning with her labor to resettle her birth-
place, Marmawell.

"One of the men who came to Marmawell to resettle the
spice fields was a tamer of wild wingwands," she said. "Once
he let me watch."

Camlach's eyes bent on her more intently. With his eyes he
touched her eyes and lips and neck and arms.

"Tell me," he said.

"The wingwand was sky blue."

"What color is the blue of the sky?"

"Just so. At times he was the grey-blue of a mountain far off, and in the turn of a wing, the deep blue of a warm sea or the green-blue of a swift river. When the wind ruffled his back hair, his color was the white-blue of a cold sky, and in the darkness of a cloudy day, he was not blue at all, but black as the underbelly of a storm cloud."

"Such a beast should be able to fly in the sky unseen," Camlach said. His eyes were lost now in the vision of the storyspell that she wove, but he could still speak. She wove it more strongly still.

"Yes, but I never saw him fly, my prince. He had been tied to the ground for many winds, for you know that such is the way in the taming. He was tied until it became an agony to him, tied until he had bled himself against the ropes, tied until he no longer fought."

"That is too long," Camlach said. She smiled wryly, but she saw in his eyes a deep desire, as a wingwand for flight.

"The day I came to see, the wingmaster mounted and cut the ropes for the first time. The beast would not fly. For a long time he tried to encourage the beast, coax it, but the beast would not fly.

"'Fly!' he commanded, and he spoke to the beast of wind and cloud and sun, and the joy of living above the earth. The wingwand did not move."

"Sky-fear," murmured Camlach.

Marwen nodded.

"Tied so long to the ground that the beast began to fear his natural domain, kept from flying so long that he forgot his wings. The wingmaster wept and told me that it rarely happens, that it is a risk with great reward. Soon the beast died."

They looked at each other silently for a moment. "It were better that man had never touched the beast," she said.

Camlach nodded and then asked, "Marwen, have you ever ridden a beast tamed from the wild?"

She shook her head.

"The wingmaster spoke correctly when he said it is a risk taken that often has great rewards. These wingwands fly so high that the air becomes thin and cold on a midsummersun day. They fly so swiftly that only the strongest riders can stay seated. They can skim the earth at the height of a man and can hover for the span of a wind. Their endurance is boundless. Their flight becomes a song; the journey becomes as sweet as the destination."

Marwen listened. She did not touch Camlach. She did not know how.

"Someday you will show me," she said.

"I will."

"In the meantime I will believe you."

They both looked down.

"Do you remember Maug?"

Camlach frowned. "I remember him. He stole Politha's blanket, but I disliked him before that. He was unkind to you."

"With the blanket he deceived the Oldest into believing that he was the wizard's heir. He read her books, even the most sacred, and with his new knowledge, he stole the prism moon."

Camlach bent his head to the side slightly.

"It is not called that around the fire. I have heard it named the 'close moon,'" she said.

Bim Staffmaker came from the shed and stood in the room as if one had summoned him.

"Prism moon ..." the prince murmured.

Camlach looked at Bim a moment as if trying to remember something. He jumped to his feet. "If you have work, I will do it for you," Camlach said.

The old man seemed pleased but gestured to him to sit down. "No, no, it is nothing. I only thought I heard someone call."

"Then come and sit. I think we shall need the counsel of your grey hairs," Camlach said. With the tenderness of a son for an aging parent, he helped the old man to sit on the greatrug. Marwen closed her eyes briefly and continued.

"He cast a spell on me—I knew it even before Lamia told me."

"Lamia." Camlach said. "The girl who watched you in the window."

Marwen nodded. "The Oldest's apprentice. She has been deceived also, or perhaps the power of the prism moon was too much for her."

Camlach looked at the Staffmaker, who was as still as a tree in lostwind.

"Was this Maug born to power?" Bim asked after a time.

Marwen shook her head, "I have seen his tapestry. There was no staff. Will you believe me, sire, and give me my staff?"

"I do not hold with this Lamia. Wielders of knives are no friend to the good magic. But this Maug—he must have some gift, or he would not be able to wield the magic of the prism moon."

Marwen was still for a time, and then she covered her eyes with her hand.

"My magic works backward," Bim said. "The wizard must obtain the staff to prove worthiness to have it." He smiled. "The staff, the wand of faerie, symbol and scepter of the spellmaker, the axis and the tally." He frowned. "I do not make the staff cheaply. It comes at a cost: the most precious gift the wizard has to give. Such giving is instructive." He gestured toward a chest, dark and solid in the corner of the room, and shuffled over to it. He lifted the heavy lid.

"Many of the gifts I have here still, collected and saved by my predecessors and myself. From Talon-ra of ancient days, a precious snowseed, from which grows a tree of white and magical fruit that produces fertilized seed but once in a thousand years. The Staffmaker of that day planted the seed, but it would not grow, and so from Talon-ra's son he demanded ... an eye." The old man held up a small glass jar in which floated something pale and fleshy. He looked at them and chuckled. "The right eye. This gift was well suited to this wizard's particular weakness. After that he could look at only one woman at a time."

He bent over the chest again. "Here is a bag of gold from Mivadlonor the second, but rarely is money required. For instance, from the wizard Tuk was required a lock of hair from the head of his dead child. You see, Marwen, it is not the staff that makes you a wizard. You will be a wizard before you come to me, and you will know. But in seeking the staff-offering, you seek the way to that knowing."

"What of my father? What was the offering he was required to give?" Marwen asked.

"Ah, your father—" and then the old man scowled, and his face was as twisted and gnarled as the knot of a tree. "Nimroth of good fame, but not in my house. He requested of me a special staff, one that would last on a long journey, one that could go with him into dark and far lands, lands of death. Of him I required a gift of great price: his son, body and soul."

The Staffmaker's voice softened, and he leaned against the chest as if he were weary. "An apprentice I needed, and still need, one with the ability to learn the art of staffmaking." He picked up one of the sticks and ran his fingers like tree twigs down its length.

"I have lived long. For three wizards I have created staffs. I have become one with the trees, but even they must have an

end. I could not have a child of my own. I was not enough of
this world. That was why I asked for Nimroth's son, for a wizard can have more than one child, though it is rarely done."
His robes engulfed him; his frame all but disappeared under
them. He fixed his eye on Marwen, gleaming, liquid-filled. "I
gave him the staff on the promise of his son, but it seems he
tricked me. Went and had a girl." The Staffmaker laughed
again, a dry laugh, like branches clacking together in the wind.
"How the world changes. I feel sometimes as if all the magic in
the world was seeping out slowly, as if the Mother was bleed-
ing to death...."

The fire was darkening, and Marwen saw pools of cold light
seeping under the door and beneath the window. She wished
he would stop speaking so she could think, but he went on.

"Your father said, 'I haven't time,' and I said, 'Nor I.' I
trusted him, but he cheated me. The great Nimroth cheated
me. I will not be cheated again. This time, you should have
brought with you the price of the staff. You should have
brought the price of your own staff and your father's also."

"What then is the gift you require of me?" In that moment
she knew she would gladly give an eye or a limb.

Bim fed the fire with a log. It did not burn slowly and gently as a rushweed fire, but with a roaring and a great heat, then
soon out. He looked her in the eyes, steadily and with power.

"I had a dream, that I should forgive you of your debt and
your father's debt if you brought to me an egg, a wingwand's
egg. It was to be a special egg, with visions in it, to tell me
where my apprentice would be found. And the wingwand that
hatched from such an egg, ah ..."

He looked at her hopefully, as if he thought she might run
out and bring it in from the snow.

"I had such an egg," Marwen said. The fire cracked and
hissed. "It ... it broke. I was hungry. I think I was dying...."

"Wingwands are few and precious here," Bim said as if he hadn't heard her. He stopped. "You did not bring it?"

"I can never bring it," she said.

He shook his head and closed the chest with trembling hands. "Then my visions are true. I am not required to make a staff for you."

Marwen listened to the wind squall against the door. She said, "But I brought it so far."

Marwen saw herself, cold and dying, on the rock face of a mountain, breaking the egg and consuming the liquid life within. She remembered how light had been her step afterward, how much stronger, relieved of her burden. Now the burden returned, like a deep private sorrow.

"I bear the egg still," she said, "as a grief within me, a spirit-thing."

Bim said nothing. He spread his mat on the greatrug as if he were preparing to sleep. Marwen swallowed hard.

"It was cold, I had no food, I would have died," she said.

"Why did you come into the mountains without food?" Bim asked. He did not look at her. "Bashag would have given you food."

"How did you...?" She stopped. He looked at her then, and his face could not have been more frightening to her at that moment if she had come upon a real tree with living eyes moving in it. She said slowly, "Bashag misunderstood my magic and thrust me out. I meant to help, but instead the spell ..."

"Ah, then you used magic in winterdark," he said. "And the snow that fell—it was long and deep for these mountains—what of that? Did you not bring upon yourself the cold you complain of, Nimroth's daughter?"

"But in pity!" she cried.

"And the visions in the egg? If it was in pity that you summoned them, it was in pity only for yourself. Ah, Marwen—

always disobeying, always disobeying. If ever you can earn the staff that balances evil in the world, it will be to balance the evil in your own heart as well."

"Not evil," Camlach said, his voice low and even. "You do wrong to call it evil."

"You needn't bother to use your royal tone with me, lad."

"Are you not my father's subject?"

"No more than the trees, and they do not bow to any king." He turned to Marwen. "You had a task to do first, is this not so? That was the first disobedience, before all the others."

Marwen leaped to her feet as if she would flee or strike out. "You do not know how I was plagued by visions and dreams!"

"What dreams?" Bim asked.

"Dreams. I do not remember," she said. "I don't see them clearly."

"If you cannot see or remember your dreams, you cannot wield a staff. It is too much power to give a dreamer of secret dreams."

Marwen fell to her knees before the Staffmaker, her hands open, imploring, but she stared at him and did not speak. All the words that had been in her mouth seemed false and foolish now. Her throat hurt her; she felt as if a hand gripped her neck and choked her.

"You and the One Mother see what I have done," she whispered. "By the gods, you must let me set it right."

Bim sat unmoving for a time. "All my days have become brief, full of faceless people and places I did not look at hard enough." He sighed. "Get me this moon," he said, and his voice shook with hopelessness. "Bring to me the prism moon, and then I will give you your staff." He lay down again and pulled a blanket up to his chin.

"But ... but I cannot do it without a wizard's staff...." Marwen said.

The wind began to hiss through the cracks in the boards of the house.

"My magic works backwards," Bim said, half-asleep. "The Mother go with you."

CHAPTER TEN

Pray for love, for in the absence of love is found evil. —NOTES OF NIMROTH, FROM A LATER JOURNAL

"I HATE HIM, I HATE HIM," SHE SAID hoarsely. She stumbled to the door of the Staffmaker's house but stopped at the threshold. The air outside was charged with the power of the spell. She could feel it lift the hair on her neck and arms. She could taste it, metallic in the back of her mouth, and the snow shone blue with it. Camlach was behind her. "Marwen?"

Slowly, she stepped into the snow, and immediately the pull of the spell overcame her. It became hard to breathe, harder to hold her head straight, harder to remember who she was and her quest. She looked toward the darkness in the south. Prism moon, the wind called, and her body shivered in pleasure and pain. How strange that the Staffmaker should send her to seek that which she most wanted. Surely this was no price, no sacrifice, she thought.

"I will come with you, Camlach, and we will descend upon Maug with armies and such magic as I have." Her voice sounded strained and breathless in her ears.

"It is what I sought you for," Camlach said, but he looked at her with uncertainty.

"And I don't have to give it to him." She gestured toward the Staffmaker's house. "The prism moon, when I possess it, will be better than the staff."

Camlach said nothing. He led her to a higher terrace where his wingwand snuffled at the snow for winter grasses.

"Dragonwing is his name," Camlach said to her, his breath making clouds in the cold air. Marwen grasped Dragonwing's long glossy backhair and tried to mount, but the animal shifted away, whickering. Again Marwen tried, and again the beast shifted away so she could not mount.

"I don't understand," Camlach said under his breath, and he mounted the beast himself to see what the problem might be. Dragonwing let him on easily.

"He has never done this before," Camlach said. "Perhaps if you let him touch and taste you...."

But when Marwen went around to the beast's head, he reared and squealed and did not settle until he was away from her. Marwen was knocked down as the animal shied. Camlach took the beast by the antennae to calm him.

"Teach it a lesson!" she cried, almost weeping in shame and frustration. She pulled at the sword in Camlach's belt.

He held her hand gently. "Perhaps it is you, Marwen," he said. She was breathing very hard.

Camlach's face was full of blue hollows. "I think Dragonwing can smell the egg on you, the wingwand egg that you ate. Neither he nor any other beast will carry you."

She knew it was true, but she hated him in that moment for saying it.

"Why did you come here?" she asked cruelly.

The blue hollows deepened to grey-black, and his eyes were lost in shadow. His face seemed far away and out of reach.

"To help you...."

"Then why don't you help me?" she cried in rage. "And why didn't you come before? I wouldn't have eaten the egg if you'd come."

"Marwen," he said, gripping her shoulder, "you keep trying not to be afraid. Your magic, your staff, even the moon—you think they will make you safe. But to hold their magic is danger."

"It is like you to think so," she said, her voice sharp and low, "you who run from your father's protection at every chance, the sheltered younger son, the one who must always break his bounds to prove himself. I suppose you think the moon will bring you adventure, what you love most. You could scarcely mourn your brother because his death meant war. Deny it! Don't I know you? Haven't I watched you in visions and dreams and let a single word tell me a thousand things about you?"

He took her chin firmly in his hand. There was anger in his touch, and something else. "And yet it is you that Dragonwing will not carry," he said.

Marwen struck his face, and her hand stung hot.

"My beast will carry you," a voice whispered from the darkness. There was a flash of movement, a hand throwing something.

At once the moonlight burned dry and red, and Marwen's eyes felt as if they were afire. She fell into the snow, blind. The sound of Camlach gasping and struggling filled her ears for a time, and then there was silence and warmth and Lamia's voice, soft and sweet. The pungent smell of shordama and the sting of it made Marwen's eyes tear.

"You will come with me now, won't you Marwen. My wingwand Leoptra will carry you to my master."

Camlach was close beside her.

"Don't listen to her, Marwen. She has dulled our minds with shordama," he said. She could see him now, hazily, his hair and face dark with powder. His eyes teared also, and the tears ran down his cheeks like blood dripping.

"I have heard your heart," Lamia said close into Marwen's ear. "I know Maug's spell has at last conquered you, for you seek the prism moon."

Marwen felt light and languid. She felt Lamia fumbling with the tapestry pouch at her side, and then the girl was gone. The snow felt warm under her, and the stars sparkled more brilliantly. She heard Camlach's voice far away, heard him stumble in the snow, calling out. After a long time, Lamia returned.

"So his price is the moon," she said. She tucked Marwen's tapestry into Leoptra's gear. She leaned down close to Marwen. Her face was ghostly in the moonlight, her lips black as blood. "Master will have his staff, won't he."

Lamia uttered some words to her wingwand and said to Marwen, "Come."

Marwen stood shakily. She could see only what was just before her eyes. First Camlach was not there, and then he stood between her and Lamia. His golden cloak was green in the cast of Epsilon's light. He was shouting something at Lamia so loudly Marwen could not distinguish the words. He blocked Marwen's way. She put her face into the back of his cloak. She smelled him, drew in deep draughts of the scent of leather and snow. She closed her eyes and let her hands learn the shape of his arms. He turned to her. Lamia was laughing.

He bent down to her, and Marwen opened her mouth to breathe in his breath. Lamia was saying something, a spell perhaps, Marwen wasn't sure. And then Camlach was wrenched from her arms. Leoptra let her mount easily, and Marwen leaned against Lamia's small soft back, so different from Camlach's. She did not turn to see who struggled and panted in the snow behind her.

THEY LANDED FIRST near a lake cupped in the valley of three mountains, its water gleaming like molten silver in the moonlight. "He follows," Lamia said to Marwen. She said nothing else. She dismounted and groomed her beast with sluggish movements. Marwen could not move at all. Lamia withdrew and built a small hot fire. She threw shordama onto the coals again and again. Once when the effects of the shordama were wearing off for her, Marwen approached the fire, but Lamia hissed at her and would not share.

"There is no need," Lamia said, slurring her words. "The moonspell is enough for you now."

Marwen was cold and hungry and no longer drugged when Camlach landed near their camp. He looked at her and without speaking built a fire away from Lamia. He went away with his bow and returned with a callobird plucked and cleaned and ready to roast.

"When you have eaten, we will leave," he said. "In her state she cannot follow us. We will take her wingwand."

Marwen slowly shook her head. "For what reason? She can take me to Maug more easily than I can get to him myself."

"You aren't truly going to him," Camlach said.

"I must," Marwen said. "He has the prism moon."

"But can you suppose that he will give it to you? It is better that we flee from Lamia and find a way to steal the moon."

Marwen was silent.

"Marwen, come not for my sake alone, but for my people," he said, and his voice had a pleading edge. "Listen to me. Some time ago the women of the palace and surrounding villages began noticing, talking together heart to heart as they are wont to do, that no babies were born without trouble and that even those who had before delivered with ease did not. 'It is magic,' they began to murmur, and eventually they asked a village Oldwife to go before the king and inquire of him what they should do.

"Oldwives from other villages traveled great distances to tell of similar troubles. My father was puzzled and sent to the Oldest in Loobhan with his problem. His messenger did not return. Again he sent, and again, and still no word. At last he sent my older brother and a detachment of men."

Camlach looked down at his hands. Marwen noticed the fingers of his hand trembling. She longed to touch them, but her hands seemed too heavy to lift.

"My brother never returned. Two of the soldiers came back, one mortally wounded, the other wounded in his soul, for it was cowardice that had saved him. 'Your son is dead,' they told my father, 'and so too is the Oldest, Shadrah.' My father in his grief wanted to send his entire army to defeat whatever evil was there in Loobhan, but the soldier advised against it. He told us that Loobhan had been conquered by a wizard, and all those who will not concede to his rule are put to death. When Torbil came he told me that he had a friend in Loobhan, an influential friend, chief of the city guards. He left for Loobhan when I left to find you. Perhaps this way ..."

Marwen smiled at the memory of her friend.

"Then you were not angry with Torbil for letting me go without you."

Camlach snorted. "I was angry. Why do you think he volunteered to go to Loobhan?"

Marwen smiled faintly.

"There is the matter of a promise I have yet to keep," she said at last.

"Ah. You promised Maug that you would be witness at his tapestry remaking." Camlach was silent for a time, looking at her. "It is true. The spell Maug has placed on you has a great hold. What of the promise of our tapestries? You will die and leave me alone, both in this world and the next."

"The other promise was first," she said. She shook her head. "How can a prince love the one who has caused his people so much pain? Do you not see how it is I who caused your brother's death? Camlach, I saw it, I saw him die. He died mad, mad for the moon!"

"As you are?" he asked quietly.

Marwen looked into the dizzying stars. She wasn't sure if she was seeing them as an illusion or more clearly than she had ever seen them before.

"We are so unalike, my prince. You dance and play your lyre at royal pageantries, and a hundred eyes more fair than mine gaze upon you. And I, I sing in the darkness on a hill, and no one hears."

"This is the spell speaking," Camlach said. "Since I have been without you, I do not sing or dance, Marwen. It is not just my desire; my whole wisdom tells me that it is right that we be together. Your sign is in my tapestry, the sign of the white wingwand."

"Zephrelle is dead. I ate her baby," she said as if that should answer him. Marwen could see winterdark flowers blooming: doddy and moongay and blueblush, grey in the darkness and snow.

"And what if we did marry? To be a wizard is one thing, Camlach. The magic flows in my veins instead of blood. I carry it with me like an extra heart. My lungs extract it from the air. I was born for the magic. But to be a queen! What could I give you? You could give me purple and gold...."

Camlach laughed. It was not a kind laugh. "My brother is

dead. I had no desire to be a king, but now it must be. This is real, Marwen. Maug has killed, and because he has killed a prince, he has changed the future of Ve. He bore no honest love for you before, though at times I saw lust in his eyes. Surely, he will kill you and claim the wizardship as his own."

"He cannot be wizard without the staff, and the Staffmaker would never give him a staff."

"But he has the moon, Marwen! He rules Loobhan with it. He has bewitched Shadrah's apprentice, all with the help of the prism moon. And though he needs no staff, he holds the price in his hands."

Marwen looked up at the sky where the seven moons of Ve shone shyly. Epsilon was very blue tonight behind the grey clouds, and Septa, half-hidden behind a mountain, lay on its crest like a cone-shaped crown.

"Look at that group of stars—there. Have you ever seen them before?" She gestured to the south horizon.

For a time he was silent. Then he stood and looked into the sky at the few stars that shone through the clouds. When he looked at her again, his face was shadowed.

"New stars? What does this mean?"

Marwen looked blindly toward the south.

"The heavens are changed because of what Maug has done, Camlach. In all Ve many babies are born sick and dead, if they are born at all. The earth also casts out her young. Little food grows, and less still will grow in summersun in the absence of the upwellings. When Maug plucked the moon, trying to keep all love for himself, he caused love to fail in the world, and growth and order to cease. Such power I have never seen. Against this, what good is your sword or my magic?"

Camlach was silent so long that Marwen looked to see if he was still there. He was staring at her.

"By the Mother, Marwen, my love has not failed."

The new magic flooded her. She closed her eyes for a moment in the wonder of it. It was like the old magic, when it filled her and led her to power and creation. Only this magic, this magic was a shared gift. It demanded that it belong to two. The spell in her heart stirred, squirming like a worm.

"You desire me as I do you," she whispered.

She wondered that she could not speak the word "love" as if her lips were now unable to form the word.

Camlach touched her hair, his fingers slid down her cheek and her neck. "My desire is not only desire, but need. As I need food and water, I need your love, Marwen. Say not that you admire or desire; say that you love."

Marwen lowered her eyes. Fear and need, both, filled her stomach maddeningly.

"I am thirsty," she said.

He was still a moment. Then taking the gourd from his wingwand's cinch, he stalked to the lakeshore a small distance away. She watched him drink and then fill the gourd for her. The blood pulsed in her throat.

"The water is good," he said when he returned. He stood with his legs apart, his back erect.

Her hands reached out for it, but he did not give it to her. "Do you thirst, Marwen?" Slowly, deliberately, he poured the water onto the grass before her. "Let me teach you what it means to thirst."

Marwen stood angrily and strode toward the lake. She did not stop at the shoreline, but waded in until the cold water slapped her thighs. She drank and waded in the lake of light until wyxwind. Camlach walked along the shore, but she did not come out of the water until he was gone.

CAMLACH SPENT THE sleeping winds under his beast's wing. He was gruff when he built the fire next waking wind.

He shouted at Lamia, "How long do you stay here, witch!" But Lamia rolled in her greatrug in a stupor. Marwen drank from the cold lake and ate only what Camlach handed to her. As the winds wore on, Camlach became quiet and then gentle with Marwen.

When next Lamia awoke from the love-slaked dreams of the shordama addict, he gave her a little cold meat. She ate it as he rolled her greatrug and tended the fire. She watched them both with her slanting eyes, but now the eyes seemed smaller to Marwen, like a leaf curled at the edges, blighted.

"How I weary of the darkness and those moons," Lamia said to them. "How I weary of you both and your childish little affair."

"Winterdark is half-over," Camlach said mildly.

"Sometimes I fear that I will never live to see another summersun," she said. "Sometimes I fear that I will." She laughed, a hard mocking laugh. Camlach laughed too, but softly.

"Where do you come from, Lamia?" he asked gently.

Lamia looked up, surprised at his question, suspicious, but Camlach's open gaze disarmed her, and she looked into the fire and answered. "I come from the seashore village of Bu, far to the south on the peninsula of Greenpoll. My talent was discovered as a child, and so, as a gift to the Oldest, I was sent to Loobhan for training. When the year was up, Shadrah kept me for another and another, and two years ago named me her apprentice when I was sixteen suns."

"Was Shadrah a kind mistress?" he asked.

Her face was still, no sneer or smile marred the beautiful features. She stared at nothing. "She was strict, and fair...." She stopped. The sharpness returned to her eyes, and the red shordama-stained mouth twitched.

"You waste my time," Lamia said harshly. "We must be on our way."

"Do you remember your mother?" Camlach asked, persisting.

But Lamia laughed shortly and walked away as she answered.

"All I remember of my childhood is how the hard ripples of the sand hurt my feet and that, to the coast of Bu, the callo-birds came to die."

Chapter Eleven

I met my lady singing by a stream,
Her hair unbound and in the sun agleam,
Shordama stains upon my lady's lips,
And red again upon her fingertips.

She smiled at me and sang a song of pain,
I promised that I'd come to her again—
Shordama stains upon my lady's lips,
And red again upon her fingertips.

I brought her ruby powders, scarlet, fine.
She told me that forever she'd be mine.
Shordama stains upon my lady's lips,
And red again upon her fingertips.

I watched my lady die beside a stream.
She swore her love for me was but a dream.
Shordama stains upon my own grey lips,
And red again upon my fingertips.
–"The Ballad of Bu Witch" from *Deathsongs*

Their flight led them further into the mountain range, the peaks higher and more heavily snow covered, until the beasts' wings carried not the sound and smells and the movement of the earth, but a cold dark dampness. They landed often for the sake of the wing-wands that had to fly in the thin air. Marwen found the air no easier to breath when they landed. Camlach's fires could no longer warm her. The mountains leaned toward her, swelled and shrank in the moonlight, mountains like kingdoms, provinces of rock upon which ridges and fields of snow lay like silver. Not just mountains, but the whole earth climbed upward as if Ve were a great bowl out of which one might fall.

And sometimes there were trees. Trees, bent and leafed on one side only, their concession to the raging winds, grew out of the sheer rock face. In the valleys were enormous trees gowned in green moss, their branches, high overhead, white with dewed mist. On some trees the trunks boiled out into blisters, and the wood twisted and bubbled into magical faces as if someone trapped inside struggled to get out head first. Marwen lost all sense of self. She became the mountains, the trees, the snow, the wind, the stars, a moon. She was huge and hard like the rocks, and soft and cold like the snow; she was distant like the stars, and love-filled and luminous as the moons; she was solid and still as the rooted trees, and wild as the wind. It was her head that thrust against the bark of the trees, her face on every one, pushing, straining, and never born. The strength of the spell grew over her heart like a caul.

She held onto Lamia, mounted atop Leoptra, as if to her own body, her sister, her other self. She would not ride with Camlach, fearful that he would take her away from the prism moon and not toward it. There was no hope of that anyway; his wingwand still would not let her come near. Lamia was grim, slumped, and unseeing, as if, now that she had her way and was bringing Marwen to Maug, she was flying toward her own death and not bringing Marwen to hers. Marwen clutched her fearlessly when they were flying but did not speak to her when they were earthbound.

Camlach fed and groomed the wingwands and tirelessly found them food. He built for Lamia, when they made camp, the hot little fires with which she burned shordama. He listened to her lurid babbling when she was intoxicated and covered her with her greatrug when she fell asleep. Marwen watched this with revulsion and a strange sense of consolation.

Once she said, "She has enchanted you too, my prince." Then she walked a distance away to where the snow lay soft and deep. She sat in it and marveled at its perfect smoothness. A little way from her, she saw a small movement on the snow, and she thought it was a bird or a flower bending in the wind. But it was a snowsnake that slithered, white and barely seen, into the snow, into its tunnels beneath the smooth surface. She jumped up and ran into the perfect patch of snow, tromping it and ploughing it and kicking it, until Camlach found her there, sweating and cold, and led her gently back to the fire.

LAMIA BEGAN RATIONING her shordama, for the pouch she kept it in began to sag and wrinkle. Camlach watched her carefully. He put his cloak around her and made her wild-flower teas when she had fits of shivering. He no longer questioned her, but told her stories of court and sang her songs and sat quietly at the fire with her, wind after wind. Once though, when her mind was her own, Camlach asked her how she came to be addicted.

"Maug gave me my first taste, secretly, when Shadrah was unaware. He said it would make me wise." She shook her head a little and smiled. "Would that I were less wise."

"You loved Shadrah, didn't you," Camlach said. "That was why you trusted Maug, because she loved him."

Marwen looked at them both blankly. The spell was like a thick fog around her by now, and the words of the others were muffled and garbled, almost as though they spoke a foreign tongue. She understood them, but her lips could not form the words to speak. She could not even force her face to appear interested or alert.

"Maug came to Shadrah the Oldest one windeven when she stood looking to the north for the wizard's heir, for so she had been promised. A stranger could be seen stumbling down the slopes to the city. She went to him. He was half-starved and footsore, and when Shadrah questioned him and saw that he walked across the wilderness and lived, she thought her promise had been fulfilled. She asked him, 'Are you him for whom I have waited? Are you Nimroth's heir?' She knew that to most people that would mean nothing, but his eyes flashed horribly. He did not answer then. Later though, after he had regained his strength, he showed us that he could vanish at will and cause rocks to heat without fire. Shadrah cared for him, grew fond of him, let him read even forbidden books. At last he shared with us his secret: he was the wizard's heir."

Marwen could not speak or move. Camlach prodded the fire.

"Did no singers come to Loobhan to tell of the deeds of Marwen of Marmawell?" he asked.

Lamia nodded. "He spoke of her. He said that she left Marmawell to burn, knowing the dragon sought her. He said that she cast changing spells on her father and tricked the Taker into robbing her adoptive mother of life. He told us how she abandoned him in the wilderness to die. When the songs came to Loobhan of her deeds with the dragon, Shadrah stopped up her ears and would not hear."

Camlach looked to Marwen to defend herself, but Marwen said nothing, only struggled to hold her head up. Her neck felt narrow and weak; her jaw trembled.

"Maug has taken truth and twisted it into falsehood," he said kindly to Lamia.

Lamia hugged her knees and rocked herself. "This I know: that Shadrah felt the magic on him, and she had a dream. She dreamt that Nimroth was comforting a woman whose name was Merva. She was the mother of his child. And in the dream he said, 'I have breathed into his soul a skill with his hands and a certain magic.' His soul, his life, do you hear? Nimroth had a son." Lamia closed her eyes and sighed. "Shadrah prayed to dream again, but nothing came. She said someone had stolen her dreams."

Camlach looked at Marwen open-mouthed, but Marwen was seeing Nimroth's lips as she had seen them in her hundred dreams, and she knew that the words matched the movements of his mouth.

Marwen felt her heart shattering as if it were ice, a ball of glass. She forced her mouth to work, the words coming thick and clumsy. "The dreams of an Oldwife are true," she said.

Lamia stared at her. "Why do you say this? Is it trickery? Why did you help Loronda when you knew it would be bad for you? Why do you touch me as if you loved me? Either you are a fool or ..." She did not finish. She looked at Camlach and then at Marwen again, and then she strode away. Marwen was scarcely aware of her. She laid her head on her knees.

"How you have changed," Camlach said, his voice edged in anger. "Do you not care anymore?"

"The spell, Camlach, it is the spell."

He touched her cheek with the back of his fingers. "I can break the spell," he said.

His touch terrified her; the stir in her bowels nauseated her.

"Let me," he said.

He slipped the ribbon from her braid and unwound the long silver strands. He put his fingers in her hair, gently at first, and then his hands, and then he gathered her into his arms. His arms were strong, and without an equal passion to balance, she felt she would be crushed. She looked up to ask him to help her, but it wasn't Camlach at all. It was an ip-lizard that embraced her. She screamed—a high scream that rang into the night.

He broke away from her, and she saw that it was Camlach after all. His face was stricken with shock and shame and confusion.

"Oh, Mother, let me die. What is happening to me?" Marwen cried. .

Camlach touched her arm from an arm's length away, shaking. "The spell," he said, "it is only the spell." He looked toward the southern stars as if he would speak to them, and then he left her.

AFTER MANY WINDS' journey, when the moons were full and filled the earth with a brilliant cold light, they came to a low mountain of gentle slope, and Lamia declared that here ended the Giants, the high mountains, and that their way would be easier and warmer now.

She need not have told her, for Marwen could feel the prism moon, close now, pulsing its magic to her as if it were her heart, far away in the hands of Maug. It sang to her, pulled at her, caressed her. She knew that she would need her wits about her if she were to get the moon for herself. She saw Camlach gazing often at her, with a look of hunger or horror, she could not tell. But it didn't matter. All that mattered was the moon.

They journeyed toward the ocean city of Loobhan in a parallel course to the coast. As Lamia had said, the mountains were gentler. The red rock climbed in swells, like the back of an animal. The snow was gone, and water slicked down the sides of the rockface and gathered in pebbly pools. They came upon small villages in the wide valleys: Keggelah, Wickedish, Sheg. The villagers were quiet, their Oldwives sullen, but it was not difficult to obtain food and shelter from them. Lamia would not allow Marwen to speak her name. She would only mention the name of Maug, and they would be shown to a house and food would be brought. The food was meager, for the famine had begun in the coastal regions nearest Loobhan. The people who attended them were pale and silent as if taken with great sorrow.

"Are you in mourning?" Camlach asked quietly of a girl in

Sheg. The girl straightened, looked into Marwen's eyes for a hard moment, glanced behind her, and answered.

"The Oldwife's sister gave birth to a baby with fire tongue. For three days we watched it choke, waiting for it to die. Finally, at last windlost, the Oldwife killed the infant. The village mourns this winterdark, and the Sunrise Festival will not be held this year."

"I mourn with you for the child," Camlach said.

"We mourn for the mother," said the girl.

"Mourn rather for the Oldwife," Lamia said with bitterness, and then she began to eat. Her shordama pouch had hung empty for three winds now, and though her appetite had returned, a light was gone from her eyes, and Marwen suspected that the girl had little magic left with which to hold her. But Marwen would not leave, for the prism moon was her mistress now.

In Keggelah the Oldwife stared at Marwen with eyes like blackened stars, and in Wickedish the Oldwife would not appear. Marwen told herself, "When I have my staff ... when I have the prism moon ... then will I heal the broken heart, cure the troubled womb." And when reality was greater than her hope, then she would watch Camlach talk to Lamia, who hovered near him now as to a smoldering fire, and she received his kindnesses to Lamia as if to herself.

They pushed the beasts past Coe-by-the-Sea at High Month, the first day of the waning moons. Increasingly, Lamia became tense and shaky in Marwen's arms. When Camlach signaled to Lamia to land before the planned time, just on the outskirts of Loobhan, Lamia complied.

They landed on a low hill from which they could see a wide valley on one side and the ocean on the other. Lamia dismounted weakly and lay down, never taking her eyes from the sight of the ocean below. She was trembling violently now, her teeth chattering.

Marwen knelt beside her and gripped her arms. "You cannot do this. I must hurry...."

"She is ill, can't you see?" Camlach said, leaning over Lamia so that Marwen must needs move out of the way. He spoke with clenched teeth, and Marwen was frightened. Something had happened that she did not understand. Perhaps Camlach and Lamia had some knowledge that she did not share. Could they not taste the moon's song on the wind? Did it not drive them mad as well? Camlach brushed the hair from Lamia's face and spoke to her. The air was utterly still but for the thin cries of the callobirds and the distant whispering of the sea. Even the wind entered the valley with a reverent quieting, until only a murmur could be heard.

"The village just past Loobhan is called Mottle-Bee," Lamia said, her face as grey as the light of Epsilon. "The Oldwife there knows my mother. Tell her ..."

"No. Tell Marwen how she can heal you."

"She is not dying. I can smell no death on her," Marwen said, and her voice sounded distant and cold. She could see herself reflected in Camlach's eyes, her face white like a moon, like a cloud, like a field of snow. He began to speak to her carefully, like he would to a child.

"Maug's spell is over Lamia too, Marwen, but he no longer needs her, and so she will die."

"I babble much when the shordama overtakes me, I see." Lamia lay back and closed her eyes. "You, Prince Camlach, will make a good king. I offer my sovereign my magic, what there is left of it." And she laughed weakly, hopelessly.

"I accept your gift," said Camlach. "Then live. Tell us what to do. Will more shordama heal you?" He took her pouch and dumped it into his palm, thinking perhaps to find a few grains of shordama. Three tiny white bones fell out.

Lamia took the bones into her hand, gripped them in her

fist. "Obtain for me a callobird, soon, while I still have strength to use my magic," she said. She began to weep, and the sound of it was horrible in Marwen's ears. She had not thought that Lamia could feel anything beyond that which her five senses communicated to her. She was sensuous and crude, though her magic seemed more powerful because of it. Her short hair revealed her neck and ears brazenly. There were no hiding places on her. Her tears were like silver that shows the slightest touch, like smoke that your hand passes through, like the sea water: bitter and elusive.

Marwen walked down the hill toward the sea. Camlach did not watch her go, for he was searching the trees for a callobird. She felt stronger now. She would leave them behind; they had brought her far enough. She would have her moon.

She had seen the ocean only once in summersun. She had bathed in its placid waters, silenced by the bay. Here on the shore near Loobhan, it was wild in the winterdark, when the winds blew harder and colder. Mountains of water crashed onto a foreign shore, onto a place of dryness, and the waves' foamy fingers, touching the sand, smooth and supple as skin, retracted, horrified, into the moving sea.

Marwen stood herself in the place where air and water had no boundaries, where the sea thrust itself up into the air in great sprays, and the air bubbled under the sea. The mist soaked her shift and cloak.

Far out, the blackness of the ocean and the darkness of the night sky could not be distinguished. Marwen felt, listening to the ocean roar its rhythmic sighs, that she had wandered to the edge of chaos, and before her was the world before the Mother touched it, black and bleak and raw. In the hills of Marmawell, the earth tempered her strength for the sake of her children, cradled them gently, sheltered their fragile dwellings, blew softly in their chimneys, bled them little streams. But here, the

One Mother walked wantonly, with tossing hair and strong thighs, and a face as much full of terrible strength as unparalleled beauty. This was the Mother's private dancing ground, this place between air and water. Here she was creator, and destroyer.

For just one moment, in the face of the ocean beauty, the spell eased, and the pull of the prism moon.

"Mother help me," Marwen whispered, and the sound of her words echoed in the moving water. "How small I am, how driven by moons and hindered by mountains am I." The words to the prayer came haltingly. Her lips were numb, her tongue swollen and clumsy in her mouth. Finally, she let the words stay in her mouth, filling her mind. "But you have given me my magic. Help me then, to do a good thing, one worthy of your gift."

Above the ocean din, she heard faintly and sweetly, on the slope behind her, the song of a callobird.

She found it without much seeking. It was trapped among some heavy vines that climbed the trunk of a tree. She pulled at the vines, wrestling with their mute strength until at last she tore them down, and with them the struggling bird. It thrashed among the broken vines, its sleek blue-black feathers glossy in the starlight, its bright red beak opening and shutting in silent terror. Marwen reached down to take the bird, but before she could, Camlach was there. He loomed over her, picked up the bird firmly, and folded it in his cloak by his breast.

She stood looking after him until his shadow faded, and she turned back to the sea. She pulled her hood over her head. Nothing was left in her heart but the strangling spell that had returned with a greater force than ever. When she heard steps approaching once again, she vowed she would spurn him.

The pain in her heart was so great that she felt no pain when rough hands pinned her arms, and another hand clamped over her mouth.

"Silence!" a man's voice said into her ear. "With one hand I could crush such a small neck as yours."

She heard other voices, men's voices, and someone said, "Welcome back to Loobhan."

CHAPTER TWELVE

There are two meanings in every tapestry: one
leads to a full and well-lived life, one leads to
ignominy and misery. Both are correct.
—*TENETS OF THE TAPESTRY*

*T*HE HOOD OF HER CLOAK WAS PULLED
away roughly.

"It's not Lamia," one of the men growled. Thick hands
grabbed her arms and pulled at her, and she struggled with all
her strength to free herself.

"More's the pity," answered another, and they all laughed.

"How do you come to have the smell of the apprentice
about you, girl?" another asked, and he brought his face close
to hers. With one hand he rubbed the hair on his face. "What
is your name?"

The hand was removed from her mouth, and she gasped for
breath. "My name is Marwen...."

The hands fell away. As if her name were a spell, the soldiers
drew back from her.

"What say?"

"Marwen is my name, from Marmawell. I come seeking the moon."

There was a deeper silence. The soldiers' arms hung limp at their sides. Their shoulders sloped downward, and their bellies fell forward.

One man said, without moving, "Do the stories say true? That you vanquished the dragon...."

"It is true," she said, thinking that she lied, for the dragon seemed like a distant dream to her.

"Run away," another man hissed. "Flee, Marwen of Marmawell! Torbil is our friend. We will help you flee from the thief of the prism moon...."

"Hush!" she said, and she listened to her own voice as she would to the voice of a stranger. She gestured toward Septa, heavy and round above them. "Do the moons not see all? And does your master not see all that the moons see?"

The chief guard looked at Marwen and addressed her but made no move to touch her. "We will take you to the master. Come."

They walked toward the city, the guards all in a cluster around her, silent, wary, leading her carefully. But she didn't need them. She could feel the moon drawing her.

To every town and village that Marwen saw, she gave a new name, a name by which she could remember the soul of it. Marmawell, in her heart, was 'dragon earth,' for the burnings of Perdoneg had enriched the soil and caused the replanted spice gardens to bloom more richly. Wreathen-Rills would ever be known to her as 'the loom,' and Sheg was 'sorrow.' As she looked down upon the port town of Loobhan, Marwen named it 'the fish.' It lay around the shore as a fish curled in death, the huts in rows like dry scales, its main road arcing above the city like a fin. Its mouth was the bay, which sucked at the sea for breath, and the masts of many boats crowded the shore like sharp teeth. It smelled of rotting fish. It was a city more than a town, crawling with the movement of people and carts and weedsheep and flocks of podhens. In the distance she could see by moonlight a dome and a spire, and she could smell the scent of market goods and manure. A bell rang somewhere. Marwen could see that it was not a wealthy city, for only a few dozen wingwands, of no special markings, grazed on the slope behind.

Like an eye, a large building filled with excessive light lay at the head of the city. There, Marwen knew, was held the prism moon. As she stood there in the dark, she thought how pale and lusterless was the love Camlach had given her next to the bright and beckoning light of the prism moon.

It suddenly pained her to know that Maug and Lamia and others had touched it and handled it. She was filled with a quiet rage.

Clouds had gradually darkened the stars, and as Marwen was led into the city, it began to rain. The buildings of the city loomed up on either side of the street, dark and square and solid, and the rain fell on their flat roofs harshly, unsettling the dust and dripping streams of mud down the walls.

The soldiers were quickly sodden by the rain. Their heads and arms hung down; their noses and beards dripped. Marwen's cloak and spidersilk clung to her, and her braid was heavy and cold down her back. She could feel the pavement through her shoes. She had forgotten the name of the friend who had given them to her.

Men stood in the open doorways of their houses and watched as she passed, staring at her silver hair and her intricately embroidered tapestry pouch. Babies tried to touch her, and children stole away and followed for a little while. The women looked out at her with eyes dark-rimmed and hollow. Marwen could see recognition in their eyes, and she knew that though the presence of the prism moon had placed them under a dark enchantment, it had also heightened their awareness of magic. They knew her.

They were like silent animals, pressing close to her like weedsheep to the feeder, but they knew her—their deliverer, their songmaker, their dreamgiver. She had no magic for them now, no dreams or songs to give. Only that which she would take: their hope and their horror, for herself; she would take their moon, their beautiful prism moon.

She walked with the soldiers in the rain until they came before the longhouse. For show the soldiers grabbed her roughly and pushed her into the building. Glowfly crystals hung from the ceilings and stood on shelves filling the hall with a flitting white light. Even so, the long hall seemed dark, for it was angular and filled with corners and shadowed crannies. Once it had belonged to the Oldest, and within its walls had been looms and beds, and it had rung with the cries of birthing mothers.

At last she stood in a long room with many people standing about like statues, courtiers they were, and their eyes fell upon Marwen. She cast her eyes boldly from one face to another. In some eyes she saw pity and fear and in some curiosity and jealousy, but in all the eyes, great greed: greed for love and adoration and worship and desirability—all those things the possessed moon could bring, and bring without price or sacrifice of any kind. They wanted it all, with nothing to be left for anyone else. Marwen would take that away from them, and for that, she knew, they would destroy her.

The guards half-pushed, half-dragged her from the lighted common room into an ante room. Someone was in the room, someone with brass-colored hair and blemishes. He was sprawled on the floor in the center of the room, face down.

"Leave us," he said. The guards vanished, but he stayed on the floor until Marwen at last said, "Maug."

Slowly, he opened his eyes. He raised his head and lifted himself painfully to his hands and knees. There was a sickness in his eyes and a terrible beauty in his face that she had never seen before.

"These many days have I worked the spell that would bring you under my power, that would bring you here." They stared silently at one another, and his pale face flushed pink around the lips and ears. He stood up awkwardly and swayed on his feet. His hair and body were unwashed. He was gaunt, starved-looking, and his lips were chapped. There were pink shadows under his eyes.

Marwen looked at him but could not speak. Had she not always loved him? How had she born their separation all these months? Presently, he closed his eyes and sighed deeply.

"Marwen, my cousin, my sister," he said. He opened his eyes and smiled brightly. "Where is Lamia?"

"Dead by now," Marwen said.

Maug nodded. "Did she say she loved me at the end? She could never tell the difference between love and pain. She brought you far enough, though."

"I told you I would come," Marwen said. "I had not forgotten my promise to be witness at your tapestry making. It will be easy with the help of the moon."

Maug laughed, and the laugh echoed throughout the empty room as in a deep well. He shook his head. The muscles in his neck were taut, and his jaw clenched, and still he smiled. He did not look at her, but Marwen could not take her eyes from him. The walls pressed in on her, and she felt the weight of them as if her very soul held them up.

"And after you have done me this great service—then what?" Maug asked. He slipped his arm into a deep fold of his outer robe.

"The gift the Staffmaker requires of me is the prism moon,"

Marwen began, but her staff had become only an excuse. "I will reweave your tapestry in exchange ..."

She could speak no more, for from the depth of his robe Maug was drawing something, something that shone light onto his face and spilled light through the fingers of his hand. It was a tiny sun, a fallen star—the prism moon.

Marwen was unaware of how long she stared at it. Only when she felt saliva running down her chin did she clamp her mouth shut.

"You want it with all your soul, don't you," Maug said.

She swallowed hard. "How is it that you have the power to wield the lady moon?"

Maug tossed the moon into his other hand, then back again. Slowly at first, and then faster, he tossed the moon back and forth between his hands. It spun and sparkled, floated and flashed. He did not take his eyes from Marwen.

"Let me tell you a story," he said. "There were two sisters who loved each other. One was named Merva and was the elder, and she, you remember, was my mother. The other was named Srill—your mother."

Marwen did not want to hear him, but she could not stop listening. Hadn't she heard this story before? She knew each word before he said it. One by one she knew them. But she had not heard the story with her ears. In a dream, then? He did not lie; he did not change one word to another one less correct. Each word he spoke was the exact one already in her head. Not whole sentences, she did not know even two words ahead, just single words, one by one, a moment before he said them.

"A man came to their village, a poet, and of a summersun wind, he enchanted them both with his songs. The two sisters loved him, and who knows but that he loved them both. But only one did he marry: Srill."

Marwen's eyes followed the moon back and forth. Hearing the name of her birth-mother in Maug's mouth was not so dreadful as seeing him treat the beautiful moon in this way.

"If you believe this," she said, "then you know that I am Nimroth's daughter and the wizard's heir."

Maug stopped tossing the moon. He held it in his one hand and with a deft movement, set it spinning on the tip of his finger.

"But let us suppose that before he married Srill, he left a child in Merva's womb, and she bore him a son—then who would be the wizard's heir, Marwen?"

Now he changed some words from her one-at-a-time memory. Not all. Not the part about the child in Merva's womb. What then? What part had he changed? But her memory only worked forward now, and she couldn't remember what he had said or what part she had known.

Like a captured creature made to perform, the prism moon was singing to her now, with notes like rain on water or wind in the grass. Shards of light showered the walls, the ceiling, the floor. Light splashed like water into Maug's face, Marwen's hands, and she felt as if they were inside a moon-spun bubble that any moment would burst. She reached out quickly, her arm darting like a serpent, to touch the moon, to seize it.

It was gone. The moon vanished, and Marwen was plunged into darkness.

Maug's voice was all around her now, coming from every direction. "Marwen, half-sister, I am the wizard's son. My mother told me these things, and I know her words are true. You know they are true. You felt her hatred for you even as a child. Grondil, the woman who adopted you, could not protect you from it. It was a hatred born of a broken heart, for Nimroth took both their hearts. I am the wizard's son, and I claim his title."

Marwen took comfort in the darkness. "I don't believe this!" she cried. His voice was all around her.

"Why didn't the dragon kill me, Marwen? When he came to Marmawell, though I hid in Grondil's grave, why didn't he smell me, why couldn't he hear the air rush into my lungs? I'll tell you why—because I was willing it so. I knew no spells, but I willed the dragon to see ... not me, but Tamal Deathsayer's baby asleep in the shade of a bush as I had seen her only a little while before. I willed the dragon to see the wingwand that flew over the grave and then Master Clayware as he crawled out of the grave. As soon as I willed it, it was done. Three lives, to hide myself. When you came back, I had forgiven you of the three people you had destroyed—how could I condemn you?

"And then, Master Clayware gave you a message from our father. Not for me, no message for me. I knew then that my mother was right, that I would have to make my own staff. All my life she said it, and I did not understand. I do now."

"For what reason has this never been told to me before?" Marwen whispered.

Maug's disembodied voice whispered into her ear: "For shame!" He was breathing hard. After a time he swallowed, and his breathing slowed. "It will all be in my tapestry. I want you to weave it with your own hands. I want you to feel the magic tell you that it is true."

"I remember no staff in your tapestry."

"Then put it in!" Maug screamed.

The floor beneath her quivered. She clutched at the air as she lost her balance even where she stood, as if she had lost her sense of up or down. Maug grabbed her hair at the base of her neck, steadying her. She felt his breath close to her face, his lips were touching her ear, her hair.

"Sister," he whispered. "Magic does not make you immortal. If you are dead, I am unchallenged. But if you help me, the world is ours. I will make you Oldest, most powerful of Old-wives."

Marwen raised her hand. She would destroy him with her magic; she would kill him with a single spell, with one word and a motion of the hand. But no word came. The magic in her heart and blood and bone would not obey her.

Maug's grip on her hair tightened, and Marwen gasped. She dropped her arm. "Your magic will not be used to destroy. But mine will, Marwen, mine will."

He tore her tapestry pouch away from her and rifled through it, throwing onto the cobbled floor her precious book. He turned the pouch inside out. "So, still soulless. I had heard you had a new tapestry, but I knew it was a lie. There can be no tapestry for a soulless one. But I have a tapestry. And you will weave it for me, sister, in a dungeon's dark."

MARWEN HAD BEEN EATEN.

She had been thrust into the mouth of the dungeon door and swallowed by the darkness of the cell. The stone walls of the cell were slimy and damp like a bowel, and an ageless earth-deep cold breathed up from the floor. In a high corner was a small barred window through which she could see a patch of starred sky.

There was a flutter of movement in another corner. Marwen whispered and between her hands the white blade of werelight appeared. Briefly it illuminated an old woman dressed in torn rags like greasy feathers, and then the werelight puffed out, burning her palm. She blew on the blisters.

"How'd you do that?" the old woman asked, coming closer. Her face was shrunken and deformed by her huge pointed nose, and the skin of her neck fell in wrinkled folds like an old pod-hen that had molted its feathers. Marwen drew back from her.

"Ol' Maugie got you, eh?" the birdwoman said. The old

woman coughed a dry laugh and peered at Marwen, closing one eye, then the other, pulling her head back then thrusting it forward. "What is your name, heart?"

Marwen blew on the burn on her hand and did not answer.

"Don't be scared, heart. When they don't feed us, there's always crawlers and flyers," the old woman said.

"I am not afraid," Marwen said sharply.

The woman peered at Marwen again, looking at her clothes, her shoes, her tapestry pouch.

"Well, then you are a fool. Heart." She spat into a corner. "You are new to Loobhan, eh? You do not know that Maug rules the city, that he has ..." She dropped her voice to a hoarse whisper, "He has stolen the prism moon."

Marwen looked at the old woman with interest.

"I have heard these things. Why is it you do not call him Master? Are you not under his spell?"

The old woman turned away from her and settled down into her corner. The rags billowed up and settled in a heap around her. She pounded her bony chest.

"The moon has few gifts for the very old, heart. I spoke out against him. I saw what he did to Shadrah. She was my friend, until Maug came. Subtle he was, tricky. Shadrah told me once—we was friends you know—she told me about her tapestry, how it told her that she would live to see the wizard's heir." The old woman shook her head, and her eyes caught a pale ray of moonlight from the barred window. "She knew she was old even for the chief of the Oldwives. Each morning she woke and swept the walk for the Taker, in case she would come. Each evening she would look toward the north for the wizard's heir, in case he would come." The old woman shrugged. "It is that way with the old, those who spend their days missing their loved ones, their nights visiting them in their dreams. Shadrah's kin had been dead a lifetime. When Maug came, claiming that he was the only survivor of Marmawell and son of Nimroth the wizard, I could not persuade her of her folly."

"How do you know that she was wrong?"

"I am not a believer," the old woman said. "Had never heard of a Nimroth, never seen a wizard. Maug, he was nothing but a soulless one. I peeked in his tapestry pouch one time, one that Shadrah made him, and what do you think I saw? Nothing. No tapestry, nothing!" The old woman's eyes became light with remembered horror. Marwen put a hand on her pouch. She thought Lamia may have taken it, or was that a dream too?

"Did you tell Shadrah?"

"I tried to. She said it was burned in Marmawell, and that I was wrong to have peeked in his pouch. She never spoke to me again. When she died, Maug brought me here, to his house."

Marwen walked toward the barred window. The moons were bright, shimmering with color, and she could hear the distant rhythmic roar of the sea. She could not use her werelight nor any part of her magic. It was cowering in a dark corner of her mind, dazzled by the desires that surged so strongly in her now that she could scarcely think straight. She was not sluggish and drowned as she had been in the mountains, but filled with a desperate energy.

"So. You are here because the prism moon means nothing to you, and I am here because for me it means too much," Marwen said.

"You are weak," the old woman said.

Marwen pulled her damp cloak about her and sat on the stone floor. "True," she answered evenly. "And yet, we are both in the dark."

THE HOURS PASSED slowly in the dungeon. Weswind seemed to blow for three times its usual length. The stones of the floor and prison walls had so long dwelt in darkness and silence that they no longer knew their names or spoke the language of their creation. The prison, the woman told her, had been built to hold wielders of evil magic, but it had held no prisoners since ships had stopped coming from across the sea, time out of memory. The room was cold, colder than the mountain camps she had endured with Camlach and Lamia, for in the mountains had been movement and light and the heat of Camlach's love, which had warmed her even when she was afraid of it. Here the weight of the walls oppressed movement until she sat still as stone herself, struggling to breathe the air that blew in but never dispelled the stink of damp and decay. The moons cast no light, but were merely a picture, a child's painting, between the bars of the window.

Through the window came the sound of gathering people and of profiteers marketing their wares, and then there could be heard much speechifying. The cheers of the people rose like a great flock of birds.

"Is it holiday?" Marwen asked the old woman, whose name was Twag.

Twag cackled, ducking and bobbing her head in merriment.

"You might say, you might say. 'Tis an execution, heart, for outside this window is the square, and in the square is a scaffold, and upon the scaffold are put to death the enemies of Maug. It is there that you and I shall go," she said, seeming glad that she would not go alone.

"But ... but the people cheer," Marwen said.

She walked to the window. She stretched her arms and was just able to grab the bars with her hands. Pushing with her feet against the walls, she brought herself chin-level with the window. The sharp rock sill cut into her forearms.

"This one spoke against Maug because he killed her husband," Twag said.

The victim lay upon the altar, her chest bared. Her mouth was wide open, and out of it came a long thin wail. With a knife a man slit open her breast and quickly removed the beating heart. Marwen recognized the man as he turned. He seemed to look directly at Marwen. The victim had time to see her heart beating in the hand of Maug, and to watch it quiver and pulse its blood over his hand and into her eyes and mouth before she died. The crowd became silent for a few moments and then louder than ever.

Marwen let herself down from the window. She felt as if the skin had been peeled back along her spine, raw to the tiniest breezes that blew in the prison window.

"A red darkness that death becomes," Twag cackled. "A red and bloody darkness."

Marwen listened to the people outside the window leaving the square, ribald in laughter, drunken and bawdy in their songs. She heard again the story Maug had told her of their sister-mothers. Though she fought against belief, each word felt like teeth in her heart.

The hours passed. No food or water was brought, and the old woman began crawling about on the floor catching and eating insects. "Like berries they taste," she assured Marwen. Marwen's stomach felt hard as rock, her tongue like flint. She fell into sleep like a pebble into deep water.

When she woke, Maug was sitting beside her, quiet and still. His hands were clasped, and his fingernails were black with dry blood. He was staring into the darkness before him.

"It is time, Marwen. Weave me my true tapestry, the tapestry Grondil never could have imagined."

The sleep had strengthened her. "There is no staff," she said.

"Then weave for me the tapestry of the destiny I have made for myself."

"If I do, the magic will leave me forever."

He turned to her. "Willingly or not, with the spellmagic I have made on you, your hands will do as I bid." He stood up. "And if you try to trick me, well, you have seen my skill with a knife."

CHAPTER THIRTEEN

Where is the wind?
I've lost the sky,
and the stars are gone away.

Wingwand blue
ever you fly
where the lakes are cold and grey.
—CHORUS FROM "FARRELL'S PRISON SONG," FROM
SONGS OF THE ONE MOTHER

IN THE PRISON, MARWEN COULD NOT FEEL the changing of the winds. She forgot that there had ever been sunlight. She could not remember how it looked in the grass or how it rinsed the winds and brightened the shadows.

It may have been days, or perhaps only hours, before the inkle loom was carried into her prison and with it a pan of water and a pan of food. It was shoved in by a helmeted guard. He paused, a silent strange movement that Marwen barely had wits to notice, before he stalked stiffly out of the prison, and the door clanged shut.

Marwen cried, "Will you give no light by which to weave?" But the door remained shut, and there was no answer.

"If you are the wizard's heir, make your own light," Twag said.

Marwen touched her palm, still tender where the werelight had burned it. The magic seemed unfathomable to her, like a forgotten childhood language, but she stood before the loom and thought that she could weave this tapestry of untruth better in the darkness and in this place where the Mother could not see.

She threaded the loom, expecting her fingers to rebel, but they were quick and sure.

"You sing no song, speak no spell," Twag said. "This is not the way Shadrah did it."

She had indeed invoked no spell, but a magic was guiding her fingers nevertheless, speeding them in their task, assisting them in skill. It was not a magic she had known before.

From her memory she knew the symbols of the star, the floxwillow, the spoon, remembering them from her childhood days when Maug had taunted her in her soulless state by flaunting his tapestry before her. She let the magic that was guiding her dictate the movement of her fingers, choose the colors of her thread, take her wrists past the point of pain and weakness to weightlessness. She leaned on the magic, and it held her up. It brought to her mind the rest of the tapestry. There was a tree, like that which grew in the mountains, with leaves of green needles, and across the center of the tree was a knife.

Her hands worked so quickly she wondered that they did not err.

Twag watched with quick birdlike movements of her head. She asked, "Are you going to do it?"

Just before she reached the corner where the staff would go, the image of the helmeted guard swept into Marwen's mind as swiftly and fiercely as a winter wind. Didn't she know that stance, that proud carriage? Didn't she know those hands? She forced herself to stop, willed her fingers to be still, struggled to control their trembling. Slowly, she raised her hands to her cheeks. For a long time she stared into the darkness. She thought she could hear babies crying in the night, faintly and far away, and she remembered the snow fields of the mountains and the slow steady conquering of Lamia by Camlach. How had he done it, Marwen wondered, and he with no magic?

"You're not going to do it, you're not, are you," Twag said.

Marwen touched the tapestry, smoothed it with her hand. After a time she smiled. And then she laughed.

She had woven the tapestry without spell or trance because she had woven the tapestry with the magic of the prism moon. She had controlled it, not Maug. She had the strength to stop. She had the ability to refuse to put the staff in this tapestry where it did not belong. She had tapped into its source, felt the beauty and power of its gift, known its light in her mind. It was hers. It called out to her. Though Maug possessed it, in this she had prevailed. She could hold the moon without marring its crystal surface, she thought, but only if she did not give away her gift, only if she did not weave the sign of the wizard into Maug's tapestry where it had never been. The blackness before her swirled as if she were under water. She would buy the prism moon with another thing, but the moon would never be hers if she gave Maug the staff. The staff and the moon—she could not have one without the other.

She forced her shaking fingers to tie off the tapestry.

"Come to me, Maug," she whispered. The magic aided her, and her knots went swiftly and with skill. The tapestry was complete. Twag watched Marwen and the prison door from her corner.

It had been many winds since Marwen had eaten or drank, and sleep had only come to her as dreams. She lifted a hand to her forehead and felt a fever there. She held Maug's tapestry in the shadow-light of the barred window, interpreting it.

She remembered the Staffmaker's words, that one needed

power to wield the prism moon. Where in his tapestry did it tell of power?

Marwen touched the symbol of the tree with the knife at its center. "So," she said, and again, "So."

Marwen's fingers ran over the symbol of the tree again and again until her fingers tingled and went numb. The tale Maug had told her concerning his birth was true. Maug was not just her cousin, but her half-brother, the son of Nimroth the wizard. Because only one could have this sign in his tapestry. No, not only one. Two. The Staffmaker, and his apprentice.

THE DOOR OF the prison cell opened. Maug's hands were fisted, his feet apart. From her corner, Twag gasped. In two strides he crossed the cell. He tore the tapestry from Marwen's hands, looked at it, and flung it to the floor.

"So now you must die," he said. "I do not know how you resisted my will...."

"Maug, listen to me: in your tapestry I have discovered the answer—you are Nimroth's son, but not for power and magic have you been born, but to be the Staffmaker's apprentice...."

Marwen was thrown to the floor, hard. Her ears rang and she felt warm blood on the side of her face. Maug lifted her roughly by the hair to her knees.

"You think I did not know this? My mother told me herself that to wield my art I must live away in the mountains, alone, becoming old and dry, brittle like the bits of wood I carve. You should have done what you were told, Marwen."

"What can you want from me that does not require that I give away my staff?" she said. The pain in her cut temple and the sickness of fever and her hunger and thirst and fatigue were swallowing her strength.

The dungeon rang with silence.

When Maug spoke again, it was with a horrible need that

made Marwen think of worms feeding sweetly on the dead.

"It is not all you have," he said. "You have great beauty and hair like Farrell of Old." Almost gently he lifted her into a standing position. She leaned against the silent stones. His hands fumbled with her braid, and he began to unravel it slowly. His voice had changed, softened.

"How often since I was a young man have I watched your hair gleam in the sunlight and starlight, and thought that you had stolen their glory from them? Did you know that I watched through the east window of your home as Grondil brushed and braided it into a polished rope of silver, and followed you behind to collect a strand that fell?"

"Twag, help me," Marwen pleaded. Twag stared with tidy jerky movements of her bald head, her rags fluttering like dusty feathers. Maug had entirely unraveled Marwen's hair, unbound her hair to her knees, and his hands were in it as a rich man might run his fingers through discs of silver.

Marwen did not think. The words forced themselves from her mouth.

"My hair for the prism moon," she whispered.

She heard him take his knife from his belt, his breath coming rapidly. He did not take his hand from her hair.

His knife was dull, and he took no care as he hewed the thickness of it, slashing and cleaving. At last, with a sharp cry from Maug or herself, she could not tell, the weight of her hair was gone from her head, and Maug held it in his hands.

Marwen left her head bowed, listening to the sound of her fair dreams fallen. She could not hear her heart.

"Give me the moon," she murmured.

Maug looked at her, stricken. He looked at the hair in his hands and then, as if he held a great silver serpent, flung it away in revulsion.

"It is not what I had thought at all," he said to her as if it were all her fault. "It is not silver thread or moonlight, but only hair. With this you thought to buy my beautiful moon?" He laughed deeply, from his very bowels, his mouth wide and all his teeth bared, and then quickly his face collapsed with a grimace.

"How ugly you are now, Marwen," he said, and his eyes were fixed with unfeigned horror. "Or perhaps you have always been so, and you have merely bewitched me. It is well that I cut your hair, for now the spell is broken, and I see you for what you are—hideous and evil."

The illness overtook her now. With a sickening lurch, the room began spinning. There were two Maugs and two old women like great birds, and the birds were coming toward her, squawking and peering at her. Marwen struggled to focus her vision and to speak, but her words were whispers and, even in her own ears, scarcely intelligible. She pressed her eyes with her fingers and leaned, shaking, against the cold wall. "If you have ever felt the love of the Mother, I beg you, give me the prism moon."

The faces of the two Maugs contorted with rage.

"Do not speak love to me. Monster! Liar! What maiden would sell her hair, even for so great a prize as the prism moon? Your true self is shown now. And so that no one will ever mistake you again, this spell I cast upon you." Marwen heard him as from a great distance.

He pulled the prism moon from his robe.

"By the power of the moon, upon your face I place a mask," Marwen felt the skin of her face tightening, "a mask of age and ugliness, dark and wrinkled, a hag's face," her skin tingled and then went numb, "and there may it stay until you die."

He touched the mask still and solid on her face. His breathing stilled, and the light of the moon was gone.

"This serves me two ways. It appears that you have gained a

little following in Loobhan. Should they come looking for you, they will never find you." And with an easy laugh, he sauntered from the cell.

The stone door of the dungeon clanged shut, and Marwen felt the fever building beneath the mask. The water in the pan danced against the dull metal with a shimmering toss of moonlight, and in it she saw Camlach, her hungry young prince, speaking to a ragtag huddle of people and Lamia, gesturing to the left, leading them to the left, to rebellion. The moon gave her the vision, but it did not give her the strength to drink.

The old woman crawled to the pan of food and picked up a bit of meat. "Ip meat," she said and threw it away in disgust.

AT FIRST MARWEN thought it was delirium brought on by the fever when the heavy door groaned open and a helmeted guard entered the dungeon, and behind him, following with spells, came black-haired Lamia in black robes. She circled the guard, whispering spells, her hands, light and quick in the language of magic, working constantly, making the magic of concealing. When she had enshrouded the guard behind strong spells, she turned to the silent stone walls and spoke to them of the cloak of night and of masks of moss and dust and veils of mist, and begged them with enchanting words to hide them from the eye of the prism moon.

"Where is she?" the guard said.

Marwen felt as if she were in a bubble of illness. Her breath was too loud in her ears; the pain in her temples throbbed like a drum.

"She's not here," the guard said to Lamia. "Maug's taken her away. Let's go."

Marwen saw through the strong spells of concealing that Lamia had woven, that beneath the helmet was the face of the prince.

"Camlach," she whispered. The name sounded strange on her lips. She was unsure if she had pronounced it correctly.

Slowly, the young man pulled his helmet back. Lamia continued whispering her spells over the bars in the window, over each insect that she found, over the dirty pans of food and water.

"Who are you?" the prince asked.

"It is no use," Marwen said weakly. "The stones are dead, they have no spirit, they cannot hear." If Lamia heard her, she ignored her, and ignored Twag who was making birdlike noises and raising her hands to Lamia. Marwen saw, though with a strange detachment, that Lamia worked with painful concentration, her shoulders hunched, her knees bent, her head thrust forward, as she touched each stone and traced it with her finger.

"By the Mother!" Camlach said, and he knelt on one knee beside her. Marwen smelled snow and leather and grass on him. He touched her hair gently, as if touching a wound, and then he touched the hard ridgy mask on her face. "What has he done to you?" His hand touched her shoulder.

Marwen's eyes flicked open. She saw Lamia bending over Twag, comforting her while the old woman clucked and sobbed and petted the girl. But it was as if they were behind glass. "Leave me ... leave me," Marwen said. She felt herself falling asleep. Camlach spoke again.

"You are my friend, Marwen, the other half of my soul. I am going to take you away."

He put his arms beneath her shoulders and hips to lift her. She woke fully. "Camlach, no! He sees you in the moon.... You must flee!" The stone walls sucked up the sound of her voice, but Lamia stood bolt upright, tense and wary, looking into the darkness, feeling the air with her fingers.

"She is sick," Camlach said, easing her back to the floor. He looked at Twag. "Has she asked for me?" The old woman shook her head. Camlach said to Lamia, "Help her."

Lamia looked down with her eyes, but her head and neck remained erect. "A wizard must cure herself. Come, we can no longer stay here. We will find another way."

Camlach bent over Marwen who was half-asleep. "Another time you said my kiss made you want to live, Marwen," and he kissed the dry lips of her mask.

Marwen felt herself falling into an ocean of blackness so deep that it made the dungeon seem full of light. She screamed for the one who could hold her from it.

"Camlach!" she cried, "Camlach!"

There was no answer.

CHAPTER FOURTEEN

I saw the Mother's tapestry,
all warp of space,
all weft of time,
and light her shuttle, back and forth—
the endless stars
her work divine.
—SONGS OF THE ONE MOTHER

*T*HERE IN THE DEPTHS OF THE EARTH,
beneath the silent stone, the heavy weight of
rock broken from a mountain's heart, cut and tamed and made
to witness the pain of those condemned—there Marwen found
the stars and moons in the darkness of her own soul, dim at
first, then more bright. She searched the pathless places of herself, alone, and along the way she found evidences that she had
been this way before: her blue sky stone, a broken lock, bits of
broken wingwand shell. Then she had traveled in circles. Now
she traveled straight and sure. She followed the curve of that
dark land until, quick and silent, a gold sun was born on the
horizon: her own sun and her own light, the day of her hope
and magic. And it was bright and beautiful, more lovely even
than the prism moon. It was there in the timeless day of that
land that Marwen became a wizard. In place of her mortal

heart moved a spirit-thing that pumped the blood but not before it had cooled and thinned it. Even her tears came dry like ether. Her passion for the moon had changed, for she had learned that indeed it was hers but that it had always been hers and that it belonged to all the earth and its creatures. No longer was her passion for that which is forbidden or unattainable. It was instead a calm sweet passion full of knowing that the moon would be hers one day and that she could enjoy its power without possessing it. Indeed, to possess it was to use its power wrongly.

But this knowledge was not enough to fight the fever—not knowing that she had to fulfill her tapestry or that she had to replace the prism moon to heal Ve, not knowing that somewhere Camlach needed her to live. It was too late. She had become a wizard too late, and she begged forgiveness of the One Mother.

At last she saw the Taker. She came without music. She bent over her in the darkness.

"My friend," Marwen murmured, and she closed her eyes again.

"O, heart," the Taker said.

Marwen's eyes opened. The prison walls surrounded her as comfortingly as a cradle, and kneeling beside her was the old woman.

"Twag?" she whispered.

"Come, heart, drink," Twag said gently, and with bony arms she lifted Marwen's head and put the pan of water to her lips.

Twag was weeping. "Shadrah—she'd be ashamed of me for disbelieving you, child. But now I know. I've lived to see the young wizard." The old woman had removed Marwen's spidersilk and had lain her naked on the cool stones. She was wiping Marwen's masked face with cool water. She had placed

Marwen's tapestry pouch under her head for a pillow. She put her mouth near Marwen's ear. "He's afraid of you, heart. That's it—afraid. Weren't afraid of Shadrah. Didn't know Lamia existed, scarce. But you he's afraid of, yes. And Lamia—she told me. The dear child. I've known since she came. A mere babe, and I thought she was lost. And would have been, she said, were it not for the young wizard, she said. Live then, heart." And she sang a hearthsong of healing, the songs mothers sang for their babies' earaches and scratched knees.

MARWEN KEPT HER eyes fixed on the barred window and the night sky behind it. She bled Septa's magic into her, filled her soul with its white and perfect light. When Septa was halved and sunken, Marwen knew she would be well one day, and when it had fallen beneath the throat of the window, she had much recovered.

Marwen began to eat the dry bread and limp vegetables that were thrown in the prison door at times. Twag refused to eat any of the food that was brought, offering it all to Marwen, breaking it up into smaller pieces for her when Marwen would not eat.

Finally, Marwen slept a sleep of great healing, a true sleep of healthful dreams and restful darkness. She awoke to hear the prison door clang shut. She lay still in the darkness, and her skin prickled.

"Twag?"

Marwen sat up.

"Twag?" She lifted dizzily to her hands and knees. Outside in the square, she could hear the swelling roar of a gathering crowd.

Marwen pulled herself up by the bars, but she had no strength to hold herself up for more than a moment. It was enough. She saw Twag being dragged into the wind and the starlight toward the executioner's stand. She did not go silently to her death as a hunted bird, but called out as a prophetess that the wizard's heir was imprisoned, that Maug was a thief of the prism moon, that ...

Marwen fell to the floor. When she heard the crowd disperse, she began to sing Twag's deathsong. Though no note of beauty could have gone forth from the thick darkness of that dungeon, yet she made music that escaped, notes plaintive and bright and ringing with sorrow. Some passersby paused briefly near the prison wall to listen to the singing before they went on to market or to temple, and those who did went home with a small love to share. But none stopped for long near the forbidding wall of the house in which Maug had interred himself. Then she sang her own deathsong, and it was sweet with sorrow and joy.

"Who is it that sings with such power as to heal my heart?" a man asked, whispering through the window into the gloom of the dungeon.

Marwen stopped singing. She could not see the features of the man with the moonlight behind him, but she knew his voice. "The wizard," she said from the depths of the dungeon, "and one who loves you."

For a long time he did not answer. Marwen wondered if Camlach believed her. She knew he could not see her.

"Torbil has a plan to help you escape." In his tone he told her a thousand times that he loved her. "But if not ..." He pushed something between the bars of the window that fell to the floor. It was her tapestry.

"If not, I have already made my deathsong," she said.

"It will be done at Sunrise Festival, when you may use your powers again freely."

Marwen could hear the sound of heavy boots marching, and he was gone.

She was still standing by the window when Maug came to her and told her that she would be executed the next windcycle. "It will be done to you as it was done to Twag. You will see your beating heart in the executioner's hand before you die," he said.

She turned and tried to feign meekness.

"Maug, grant me one wish. Surely Sunrise Festival is only a few windcycles away. Could it not be done then, so that I might see the sun before I die?"

He touched the ridges of her mask. "It pleases me to see you beg. Very well, Marwen, you shall have your wish—almost. You will die just before the moment of sunrise."

Marwen glanced toward the window and then down at her hands. She could not speak, for she knew her voice would betray her hope.

He came closer. She could smell heavy perfume on him and wine on his breath.

"You will not escape, Marwen," he said simply.

She did not look at him. She measured the length of time between her heartbeats.

He touched the place between her breasts, traced the line where he would cut her. There was a kind of pity in his touch.

"I know," he said. "I know that Camlach has come, that he has promised you that he will free you. I would have captured him by now but for the betrayal of that witch Lamia, who is alive after all. But do not hope, Marwen. It degrades you. Hope degrades."

Marwen listened to the pauses between her heartbeats, to the silence of her body like death. "Every other moment, when my heart does not beat, I am dead," she thought.

He reached into the folds of his robe and took out the beautiful ball of moonlight, sparkling and candescent still, but it was dimmer than before, and it glowed with a reddish cast.

"Or perhaps there is one hope," he said. "A trade. Your life for theirs."

He held the moon up before him, between her face and his, and a light flickered deep in the core of the moon as if it trembled.

"Perhaps the moon—for Lamia and Camlach," he whispered.

Marwen felt a great agony emanate from the moon's bright spirit, and awful images filled her mind, specters of fruitless fields and salt-bleached shores, apparitions of mothers without milk and babies with fire tongue. She saw Loronda's child, older now, his face full of sweetness, his eyes without learning.

Marwen shook her head, and the moon was gone.

Maug shrugged and left the prison, closing the door quietly.

Marwen huddled in Twag's corner.

CHAPTER FIFTEEN

Bones, fresh-dug from the earth—strange tubers,
What death hath been sowed in thy birth?—
strange harvest. –FROM *DEATHSONGS*

AHUGE CROWD HAD ASSEMBLED IN
the square, awaiting the first hint of
dawnmonth, and the execution, for then the Sunrise Festival
would begin. But for Marwen there was only the wind and the
starlight. It was not the scaffold, black with blood, that Marwen saw as she was led to it by two hooded guards, or the faceless hordes that parted for her, touching her with their dry
stony eyes, but the fading night sky, luminous with starlight
and moonlight, and the wingflash of a white and gold wingwand as it caught the rays of the coming sun. She did not smell
old blood or sweaty unwashed bodies as she was led to her
death, but clean endless oceans and the scent of dawn-bloom-
ing goldpetal. She did not hear the knife scraping on the stone
or the old woman weeping, but the sound of children laughing
and somewhere the music of an Oldwife singing. In her last

minutes of life, Marwen would not mourn her death, but would celebrate that which would go on living in her soul.

Bright and vivid were her thoughts as she stood before the scaffolding when Maug appeared atop it. She smiled at him, and his own smile faded in the triumph of it. He went to sharpening his knife.

"Truckle up, grandmother," said the guard at her side, and thick black-haired arms hefted her up to the platform. The mask had been on her face so long that it had become a part of her, but she remembered it with renewed loathing when the guard called her grandmother, and she was filled with an urgency to die as herself. Marwen touched the mask, ran her fingers over the lines and wrinkles hardened like hide. She looked out over the crowd.

Perhaps somewhere in that mob was a prince who had vowed to rescue her. She smiled wryly and thought perhaps she had waited too long to be rescued by a handsome prince. How could he know that the moment of her death would come before sunrise, before she could use her magic? Or that she would not use her magic to save herself even one moment before sunrise? Could he guess that at last she had learned that she was not better than the littlest laws, and that from the moment one chose to obey, all the past disobediences turned to good? Only the stakes went up each time. "My life to be a wizard," she thought.

Maug grasped her spidersilk and poised his knife before her heart. "As easily as I cut your dress," he said, "so will breast and bone part beneath my blade." He punctured the spidersilk and smoothly the knife began to slice the front of her gown.

"Stop!" a voice cried from the crowd. A woman's voice it was, filled with magic and authority, so much that Maug froze and turned to the voice. The crowd fell silent.

"Speak again, you who dares to stop the moon-bearer,"

Maug said. The crowd quavered beneath his gaze and shrank back. Even the voice sounded less sure when next it spoke.

"Is it not law that one who is condemned to death is given a chance to speak?"

Marwen felt a prickling cold on her chest where her dress was cut. It was Lamia's voice, strong and undulled by shordama.

"That is the law of Shadrah the Oldest, who is dead," Maug shouted. He searched the crowd as did Marwen, but the voice seemed to come each time from a new direction.

"That is the law of the One Mother," the voice answered from the crowd, and there was a murmur of agreement that sounded like the wind in the grass.

"This is a soulless one, a sorceress who has no tapestry. Look!" He tore Marwen's tapestry pouch from her and opened it to the crowd, expecting a hiss of horror. When it did not come, he looked and saw within the pouch the tapestry. He flung it aside. Marwen thought she could hear his heart beating.

"Let us see your tapestry, Maug Moon-bearer," Lamia's voice came again. She was still concealed in spells of hiding. Maug gestured to some guards, who cocked their bows. He seemed to shrink a little in his robes, and briefly Marwen saw him as he was, a young man her own age, with blemished skin. He walked around her, putting Marwen between the crowd and himself, and placed the long knife against her back.

"Speak then, old woman," he said aloud, and to Marwen he whispered, "and be quick."

He looked nervously toward the horizon and pushed her forward roughly. She teetered on the edge of the scaffold. Even with the blade pressing against her back she felt death slipping from her. She closed her eyes and whispered to herself, "To disobey the Tenets of the Tapestry is to tip the future

away from the good magic and toward evil." She opened her
eyes. It would not take much tipping to help that knife into the
flesh at her back.

She felt herself grow chilled at the thought, and in the chill
her thoughts became calm.

There was one spell that she could weave without error: the
storyspell. She lifted her voice and spoke: "Once Princess Gaya
of old waited, as you wait, between the birth of the sun and the
death of night. Her prince, Barad, had been wounded in battle
against invading nations from across the sea, and though the
wizard Morda-hon could not heal him, for the wound was terrible, he promised Gaya that if she could keep her prince alive
until summersun, he would live."

Marwen swallowed. The crowd looked up at her with a
thousand sliding eyes, white as moons. She willed her tongue
to weave the spell. "Then the wizard Morda-hon gave her the
gift of the storyspell and went away to help with the battle.
Love had wed the souls of Gaya and Barad, so she knew that if
Barad died, she would follow. She feared this because of the
child she carried within her. So she began to weave a tale, in
the hearing of the prince, of a young man of royal blood,
beginning with a tale of childhood that sounded strangely in
her ears like the childhood of her husband, Prince Barad. The
words spoke themselves in her mouth so that soon she realized
she had no control over the way the story went. At first she
rejoiced, for she saw the prince's pain ease, and his eyes filled
not with coming death, but with desire for the next word. She
told of the boy's first ride on a wild wingwand, his first hunt,
the day he fell in love. And then Gaya began to fear greatly, for
the name of his true love was Gaya, and she knew that she told
a tale not only similar to Barad's life, but his very life indeed,
and struggle as she might, she could not control the words.
Closer she came to the present day, closer to the day of his

wounding. Tears washed Gaya's face, and Barad broke into a sweat. At last the storyspell spoke his terrible wounding, and Gaya wept sore, sure that the storyspell would speak the death of her beloved before the cupplehorn sounded the sun. It had control of her tongue but not of her hands, and as she described in great detail the mortal nature of the prince's wounds, and as the prince's eyes grew great and round, she took from Barad's belt his dagger and pressed it up beneath her heart. With all the strength he could summon, Barad stretched out his hand to stop her, but Gaya moved out of his reach. Still the story spilled from her lips, each word coming closer to the death of her prince, and so she pressed the knife harder against her breast, so that she pierced the skin. Just as she was about to thrust the knife ..."

A cupplehorn sounded, a long triumphant note that made the wind tremble. Marwen saw a sunpillar gleam over the edge of the world and fill the dark sky with a soft grey-gold prelude of light. She waited for the people to hug each other and shake each other's hands and kiss each other and clap and call and sing. She waited for them to do what all do in Ve, from end to end, on the rising of the sun. They did not move.

"Your storyspell means nothing to me," Maug whispered, but Marwen knew he lied, and that he too struggled against the spell, that as Gaya's knife would ever be on the verge of thrusting, so would Maug's.

The faces did not turn toward the sun, but continued to gaze on her. One was a deep-hooded face—the face of one of the guards. He smiled at her, and in the new sunlight, the magic returned to her and the memory of a thousand spells.

"Use your magic, Marwen of Marmawell," Lamia's voice cried out.

The voice of the crowd billowed out at the speaking of that name and built to a clamor. "Marwen of Marmawell, the Dragonslayer, the White Wingwand, Dreamgiver." The whisper of her many names filled the sky like a song.

Maug screamed over the clamor. "You know that Marwen of song and story is young. This woman is old and ready to die for her sins...."

"No!" cried Marwen. "I am young." The crowd murmured and pressed closer. "You have been too willing to be helpless before another magic. Are there believers? Then see!" And with that Marwen reached up and grasped the mask. It moved beneath her hands. She closed her eyes and whispered, "Mother, give me back myself." With both pain and relief, she pulled the mask from her face.

The storyspell was broken.

A storm of cries and shouts broke out over the crowd, and the sea of people began to undulate, heaving itself toward the scaffold, breaking its swells against the walls that surrounded the market.

Maug touched the moon within his robes with one hand and raised the knife above Marwen's back with the other. A guard, the one standing beside Camlach there at her feet, drew an arrow from a quiver beneath his robes. She saw him fit his bow. She saw his arm, dark and thick and strong—she had seen that arm draw and shoot an arrow before. Torbil. She saw him pull back and slowly, as slowly as the knife was falling toward her back, let fly an arrow that pierced Maug's heart.

Maug did not fall but stood, grey-faced. He stared into the rocking crowd as if the arrow was not still in his breast, the blood bubbling out around the arrow's shaft. "You!" he cried to someone in the crowd. He raised his arms and flung with full force his knife into the crowd. Marwen did not see where it landed. There were no screams. She leaped into Camlach's arms.

"Good thing you haven't been eating too well," he said, catching her, faking a grimace.

"Where are my bows?" Maug was shouting. "Now! Now!" His guards let fly their arrows.

"For Prince Ronor!" shouted Camlach in return. From various points in the crowd bows were lifted up in answer. Marwen saw the arrows of Maug's men glimmering in the dawn light like wire in water, saw them arcing down onto the screaming crowd. With a word she changed the arrows into long streams of water. Screams turned to shrieks of laughter and delight.

"Good people," Maug was saying, trying to silence the crowd. "Good people of Loobhan! Some among you question whether or not I am the true wizard. Look then and judge for yourself if any but the wizard's heir could do this!" In that moment Maug's body disappeared, and only his head was visible, floating above the ramp of the scaffolding. The head smiled as blood pooled in the corners of its mouth. The people exclaimed as one, and then the noise died away to an almost perfect stillness.

Marwen was standing with Torbil's arm around her protectively. With a brief prayer, she clasped her hands, then pulled them apart. This time the white flame of the werelight felt cool between her palms. She leaned forward, touching the white magical flame to the invisible blanket, and in less than a breath, it burned, leaving a faint odor on the air and Maug visible.

"I am the wizard's heir, Maug," she cried, and her voice carried and was taken up by those around her.

Camlach leaped onto the scaffold to face Maug, who stood still, his hand in his robe. He was smiling with all his teeth, and a pink foam seeped from between them and onto his lips.

Camlach flung his hood back from his head, and again a stillness settled over the crowd.

"Give Marwen the moon," he said.

Blood drooled from Maug's mouth. His face was a glossy grey, his lips blue, and he hunched over a little.

"You cannot force me to give away the moon," Maug said. "Not your brother and not you." He turned toward Marwen. "With the last effort of my life and my magic, I will put this moon far from you, where no one, not even a wizard, will ever find it again."

"You will not use the magic of the prism moon from this time forth," Marwen said.

Sweat poured from Maug's forehead and temples like tears, and slowly, slowly the smile faded from his lips.

"How can you command me—you have no staff."

"The staff is the symbol of my power. But it was in your prison's dark that I became a wizard. You will give me the little moon."

Maug fell to his knees, and his left hand, still within his robes, shook with spasms.

"I hate you," he said.

"Speak true," Marwen commanded in the language of creation.

"I love you," he whispered, gagging on his own blood.

Marwen nodded. He pulled his arm at last from his robes. In his hand the moon was a dusty diamond, a chunk of broken glass, and within it was a dull, red, throbbing glow that pulsed feebly as a dying heart. He handed the prism moon to Marwen. As it left his hand, Maug died.

The crowd fell back with a murmur. Marwen held it up to the Mother, to her sky and her pale daughters, the stars, and to her almost invisible moons, the handmaids of the earth. In her hand it cleared and shone and burst out a new blinding light, resplendent, dazzling, and the air exploded with the cheers and cries of the mob.

Camlach was smiling and looking at her. With both hands she held it out to him, to show him. An arc of white light whispered from the moon and touched Camlach's right hand, then disappeared. A cry was growing louder among the people. "Cam–lach, Cam–lach," they cried.

He held up his hands, and the roar of the crowd fell to a low rumble.

"Citizens of Loobhan, my people," he called out. "The rule of Maug is over. Marwen of Marmawell, the wizard's heir, will soon name the Oldest. Return to your homes, renew your devotion to the magic. All is well."

The crowds thinned out slowly, to celebrate with their families and friends in their own homes. Among those who lingered was a joyous festive air. Camlach put his hand up to touch Marwen's hair.

"I am not what I was," she said to him. But he shook his head and said, "I loved you by sunlight; I loved you by starlight." He kissed her, and this time she found a passion equal to his own, and she was not afraid.

The shadows were dispersed by the light of the prism moon: she had no desire to possess him, to possess even the love she felt for him; she would not wait for him or expect him to give her life or love or happiness. All this had been shadow and spellcraft in her heart. She would hold his heart lightly but with care, as she held the prism moon. Into her euphoria came the sound of Torbil cursing fiercely. He gestured to the prince. Camlach ran and bent over a clot of black shadow beneath the scaffold where Torbil was. Marwen went to his side and saw that the shadow was Lamia, lying on the ground, thin, as tiny as a child beneath her black robes. Blood pulsed feebly from a wound in which Maug's knife still protruded, erect and triumphant.

"Will a callobird save me now?" Lamia whispered to Marwen with lips no longer red, but grey as the dawn sky.

Marwen answered as she would an Oldwife: she shook her head. Immediately, the fear left Lamia's eyes, and a fierce dignity filled them.

"It was Camlach who taught me the good magic that was in me. Not all his love for me was in powders and spells. When you wish to be proud, Marwen, remember that. Nevertheless, it was your deed in healing Loronda that helped me to see my delusion, and in finding the callobird, you broke the spell I labored under. Before I die then, Wizard, interpret for me my tapestry."

Camlach handed it to her. What had happened between them while Marwen was under the spell, she knew now. Her prince could not defeat the magic of the moon, but he had used love to tame the spell in Lamia. Somehow he had known that there was a power in all the loves of the heart. She opened the tapestry and saw in the upper right hand corner a tree and within it a knife. The rest of the tapestry was stained beyond recognition, blood red, with shordama.

For a time Marwen wondered if Lamia and Maug had known that they shared the same sign. She wondered what lives they might have lived if Maug had loved and not hated— and then she left off judgment and spoke the truth that the One Mother gave her.

She put her hand on Lamia's forehead.

"Go proudly to your death. You are the tree. Your tapestry I proclaim fulfilled."

Lamia smiled faintly, and then Marwen heard the Taker's music.

CHAPTER SIXTEEN

...if...
—Songs of the One Mother

THEY WERE WELCOMED INTO THE HOUSE of the Council chief, where Marwen bathed herself two times before she would eat. Camlach served her and would not let Torbil speak of things until she refused even one more bite.

"When we walked among the people, telling them of Maug's deceit, they believed us because the people believed in you," he said at last in his deep gravelly voice. "I didn't remind them that you were a mere slip of a girl."

"Thank you, Torbil," Marwen said, smiling.

"It was Jortha, the head of the guards, who helped me, gave me and Camlach positions on Maug's execution guards. That was where we figured we'd see you next."

"Do you think you may have been cutting it just a little close, Torbil?" Marwen asked, remembering the smell of blood on the scaffold.

Torbil nodded gravely. "That is what Camlach kept on about. So I kept him busy talking to the people. Lamia put spells of hiding around Camlach as he went from house to house receiving their fealty. The people grieved with the prince for the death of his brother and swore to remember their loyalty if ever Marwen of Marmawell was brought to the scaffold. Those who did not believe were sworn to help in any case. I didn't believe it was you at first. Thought prison might age you some but not that much." He laughed, then sobered quickly.

She looked at the prince, who sat with bowed head.

"Lamia saved my life," she said.

Camlach raised his head. "She killed Leoptra, her wingwand, and sprinkled her blood on the scaffold. 'To save the white wingwand,' she said. She said it was an ancient magic. Because of it she was close to death even before Maug's knife found her."

"The deathsong I make for her will be remembered and sung always," Marwen promised Camlach.

Free of the spell, the city of Loobhan became a city of feast and dance, song and worship, and within three winds of first dawn, many ships set sail with their nets. Marwen married the couples that had waited through winterdark to be lawfully wed in summersun, and she gave each the promise that they would know one another in death's lands. She made her strongest spells for the babies born in Loobhan during Maug's rule and made many of them whole. Last of all she sang Lamia's deathsong, made more beautiful because she bore the prism moon. When all was done, she looked to the north and remembered her other promises. And her staff.

"But how can I go?" she said to Camlach as they walked the beach in the sleeping winds. "No wingwand will carry me."

"I have already thought about this, and I have an idea," he said. "Come."

He led her past the ships bumping together gently on the water and up the northern slope behind the city where several wingwands grazed. There, lying on the grass, not eating, not moving, not, Marwen feared, even breathing was a wingwand of extraordinary size and beauty. She was white, even in the soft rose light of dawnmonth, but coming closer Marwen could see that she shimmered blue and pink and green and yellow, depending on the movement of the wind in her wingscales. And coming closer still, Marwen could see that her hind foot was shackled to the ground and that her antennae were uncovered.

"She's being tamed from the wild," Marwen said with disgust.

"A wingmaster gave her to me," Camlach said. "She was tied too long, but he said that if she flies, she will be the greatest steed in all Ve. He said that the wild wingwand would not unseat you for your deed, for they know starvation; death is not so far away from them that they cannot accept it."

Marwen walked around her once, twice, and then touched her. Her antennae quivered at her touch. She was alive. She was tortured, despairing, dying, but alive, and Marwen wept as she ran her fingers through the long white backfur of the beast. At last she mounted her. She nodded to Camlach to cut the ropes.

"Will you carry me, beautiful one?" she whispered.

The beast did not move.

She did not even stand.

Marwen began to sing her Zephrelle's deathsong, thinking that she was all but dead. As she sang the beast began to stir, but still she did not fly. Marwen spoke a spell of healing, of hope. Camlach looked on, his arms folded across his chest, and his brow furrowed deeper. Finally Marwen dismounted. "Fly away then good beast. Fly home."

Marwen turned to leave, but Camlach would not. She stood beside him and watched him watch the wingwand. After a time the beast stood. "Look!" Marwen cried. The wingwand lifted its wings and rose into the air.

The force of the air beneath its wings pushed Marwen back. The wingwand flew overhead into the paling sky, circled once, and then descended to the hill near Marwen. She grazed silently, and then looked at Marwen expectantly.

When she was mounted, the wingwand lifted into the air. Marwen felt the drag and dance of wind, and she laughed aloud. Soon Dragonwing joined them, and the wingwands faced each other, their wings almost touching in their airborne ballet, and then they flew as swift as the wind over the mountains.

TORBIL STAYED ON to help in the healing of Loobhan. He could not travel with Marwen in any case, for though other wingwands no longer smelled her sin upon her, Tympanoo never forgave. So Marwen and Camlach flew to the mountains, to the house of Bim Staffmaker, alone.

"And so you have accomplished your quest, Marwen," the Staffmaker said. Marwen thought he looked older still, as if the edges of him were tattering like a cloud that had rained its fill. He was thinner, less visible to the eye.

Marwen drew herself up tall in the pride of one who has paid old debts. "I have bought the staff at a heavy price, a price that will pay for both my staff and my father's staff, for though he was a man of his word, you will not have your apprentice."

She showed him Maug's tapestry, but he pushed it away.

"Yes, yes. Do you not think that even here the story has been told? Where is it? Where is the lady love?"

"I have it," she said. "You may see it, and you may touch it, but I must return it to the One Mother."

The old man scowled. She saw him swallow his hopes before he said, "You speak as a wizard."

Marwen held out the lovely little moon of light to the Staffmaker. He shook his head.

"I don't want it. Return it to its place then, Wizard Marwen, if you have the magic to set it in its proper orbit in the heavens."

THERE WAS NO ceremony when she received her staff. Bim did not speak or scowl, but quietly handed to her the tall straight limb of a tree, strong and intricately carved with symbols and stylized runes, and filled with a white hot magic.

He would not be thanked. "Find me an apprentice with this," he said gruffly, but his face betrayed his pride in his work. "My finest," he murmured. "Each better than the last."

In the staff was a wingwand in flight, moons in every stage; there was a tree and a key and a thousand flowers of the summersun and the winterdark; and among the flowers she would find, years later, a tiny, thin, jewel-encrusted crown. There were things in the staff she did not understand, things for a future time, a destiny she had yet to explore, if she could ever believe in a single destiny again. Maug had taught her about the "if" of god. The Mother had spoken it herself in the Songs. Such a little word was easy to ignore, but Marwen would not ignore it. There was only one blemish on the staff, the swelling of an unborn leaf, and Marwen wondered for it seemed to quiver with life. Though the staff was sometimes as heavy as lead in her hand, sometimes it was as light as a feather. She loved her staff.

As well, there was no pomp when the moon was replaced. It took no magic. She spoke no spell. She remembered that she had seen the One Mother striding with the wind, still in her youth and in her long ages of bearing, indulging in her ragings, submissive to laws no man understood. But the enormous enchantment that was in Marwen's mouth could not fit into the little spells that words were. The moon floated with its own magic, spun with its own spellsong, flew on its wings of light until it vanished out of sight. In the silence after, the whole earth seemed to breathe again, and to move and push again toward her infinite labor, her continuous birth. And still later Marwen thought she heard music as a thousand women's voices filling the air, breathing out joy as a holy wind.

At Sheg, the people sent her away with quiet smiles and soft hands saying, "We have made a friend of the Taker." At Keggelah and Wickedish, the Oldwives claimed that their tears had strengthened their magic and asked that they save the blessings of the wizard for a needier time.

As they flew into Wreathen-Rills, the first thing Marwen saw was the little girl Tiu running toward her over the marshlands, her hands reaching toward the wingwands. When they had landed, Tiu embraced Marwen.

"You have your staff," she said.

Marwen nodded. The little girl seemed to have grown.

"Is it wonderful?"

Again Marwen nodded. She knelt on one knee before the little girl and grasped her shoulder. It was no wonder she had been able to see Lamia's evil and hear her words. There was certain magic about the girl. Marwen listened to the Mother.

"Did you get your snow, Tiu? Good. But remember that you would not tell me your biggest wish?"

She nodded her head. "Mama says that it cannot be...."

"If I tell you what your wish was, will you believe that it can?"

Tiu did not move.

"In your heart you have wanted to be an Oldwife; is it not so?"

She laughed at Tiu's expression.

"The Mother tells me it shall be as you wish."

Tiu ran with the wind toward her mother's house, only stopping long enough to look back and beckon to them to follow.

And so Marwen first went to the house of Loronda Toymaker. She found Loronda strong and well and radiant, and she was welcomed into her house, away from the gaze of those who followed and stared at the new wizard.

"This is my son, Ronor," Loronda said, gesturing toward a baby lying on the greatrug, his head lolling. She smiled and pushed Marwen gently toward the baby. Marwen knelt.

She held his hand and called his name softly. She swallowed hard.

"His eyes are empty."

Loronda smiled and knelt on the other side of the baby.

"Look more closely, Marwen," she said. "Bashag in her blindness has taught me this: there is no judgment in his eyes, no understanding of things mortal. But see ..." her voice dropped to a whisper, "see ... there is a light."

Marwen bent over the baby. At first she saw only his mother reflected in his eyes. And then she saw deep within the pupil a glint, a gleam of light within the deep black darkness, a tiny swirling point of light.

"How Bashag found it, I do not know. But she has helped me to realize that it is both better and worse that Ronor was born," Loronda said to Marwen without taking her gaze from her baby. "Worse because of the sadness and suffering he has brought, better because it has taught my heart a new love. I have known pain. It is a fine teacher, if one will learn, and I have learned that though Ronor does not know, he loves."

Marwen interpreted the tapestry for Ronor and discovered that the twilight-grey she thought she had seen long ago at his birth, was really a grey made by many colors. Marwen and

Loronda embraced and spoke of their sisterhood and of Tiu's apprenticeship before Marwen said goodbye.

And so Marwen came at last to the home of Bashag Old-wife. She called at the east window, but no one answered. She let herself in and found the old woman upon her sleeping mat. The tricky broom was sweeping the floor.

"Go away. I am old and weak, and my magic is nothing," Bashag said.

"Rise, Bashag. You are needed," Marwen said, placing her hand on the old woman's head. There was no sickness there, no fever, only the quick wise mind of a great Oldwife over-whelmed with grief. "It is you, Marwen. Thank the Mother, for now I can die. I was blind with pride, and though I did not send you to your death as I had feared, now I am blind indeed, and I cannot endure my shame."

"I will try to heal you," Marwen said.

The old woman shook her head. "I tried collecting back all my magic from the hot springs to heal myself, but it didn't work."

Marwen was about to work a spell when she remembered the slow magic that led a wise hand over time to grow a better seed, that gave a mother a more careful eye and taught her the magic in an ordinary pot, that led a young girl to discover that the man she loved thought her long nose beautiful.

"Get up, Bashag. You have work to do," Marwen said again. Bashag turned to Marwen with her blind eyes and then turned away.

"I can do no work," Bashag said, and the broom fell to the floor with a clatter and was still.

"You see what is true," Marwen said, "what is real and present before you. You do not look to the future with fear. Now you must not look to the past with sorrow. Bashag, I will name you the Oldest, queen and priestess of your order."

The old woman reached out her hand, her lower lip pouting out and trembling, and touched Marwen's hair.

"You are changed," Bashag whispered.

"I am a wizard," Marwen answered.

"To hear you utter those words ... I—I had despaired...."

Marwen did not answer, and the old woman sat up slowly. The broom leaped up and settled itself in its corner by the hearth.

"I am too old now to deny what I have always believed. Give me this honor, Wizard Marwen. With the Mother's help, I will do as you ask."

The naming was done in Loobhan, and there they celebrated the remainder of the Sunrise Festival. In the first rays of sunlight, the whole earth rang with the cries of her children as one song. Marwen lifted her hand in the new sunshine, the deep red sunshine, and Camlach kissed her palm.

All during Festival they circled each other like twin moons or stars, filling their bodies with the heat of the sun, sharing their dreams in sleep, and walking together in the meadows and mountains of Verduma. There, Marwen held Camlach's head in her lap when he wept for Lamia, and Camlach sang with her when she mourned the brother she had never truly known. They were seen everywhere together, and people secretly made songs about them. Merchants, when they saw the prince and Marwen, cast their wares for free, flung dainties like seeds, pressed little dolls into the palms of passing children. Musicians played strange lullabies, and jugglers tossed balls and brown eggs above the heads of the watching crowds.

Toward the end of Sunrise Festival, as they walked together, he lifted her up in his arms and held her lightly.

"And now, will you marry me, Wizard Marwen?" He spoke it boldly to disguise his fear that she might not answer him.

"But what have I to give you?" she asked, teasing, but it was cruel, and she did not smile. She begged forgiveness with her eyes.

"This," he said, and he kissed her and kissed her again, and from that moment she denied him nothing, but gave him all that he asked and all that she could give, and more, and more, and she held nothing back from him. She found that after all she could give, still her heart was more filled than ever, and Bashag betrothed them on the last day of Sunrise Festival.

BEFORE THE NEW south stars faded, Marwen numbered them and named them. She mourned long and deep for the sky that was forever changed, trembled each winterdark at the sight of the new stars, but it is said that before she was old, she learned to delight in them and taught her children a new winterdark song.